Felisa strugg
drawing the o

The earthy scent of sun-heated soil and foliage swept over her, causing her stomach to churn. She couldn't get sick now.

As she reached for a lettuce head, another contraction stabbed her. Panic filled her as the man moved closer. She couldn't afford to lose her job, and she sent up a prayer that God would help her bear the pain until he passed. She puffed to control the twisting anguish that seared inside her as the man's shadow fell across her and stopped.

"Are you ill?" His raspy voice hovered above her. "*¿Está usted enferma?*" he repeated.

She didn't look up but only shook her head.

He didn't move.

Tears ballooned in her eyes and escaped to her cheeks. . . .

The man lowered his hand and tilted her face upward into the glaring sun. She flinched with his touch and closed her eyes to the brightness, but when she opened them she saw only concern in his eyes. His gaze left her face and lowered to her bulging belly she'd tried to camouflage with an oversized shirt. "Pregnant," he muttered then lifted his gaze to her face. "*¿Está usted embarazada?*"

She tugged at her top to cover her belly and ignored his question, but she felt her face go pale.

"You're in labor."

GAIL GAYMER MARTIN says when friends talk about events in their lives, they often stop short and ask, "Will what I'm telling you be in your next novel?" Gail only smiles. Sometimes it is but with a twist. Gail feels privileged to write stories that honors the Lord and touch people's hearts.

With forty contracted books, Gail is a multi-award-winning author published in fiction and nonfiction. Her novels have received numerous national awards, and she has over a million books in print.

Gail, a cofounder of American Christian Fiction Writers, lives in Michigan with her husband, Bob. When not behind her computer, she enjoys a busy life—traveling, presenting workshops at conferences, speaking at churches and libraries, and singing as a soloist and member of her church choir where she also plays handbells and handchimes. She also sings with one of the finest Christian chorales in Michigan, the Detroit Lutheran Singers. To learn more about her, visit her Web site at www.gailmartin.com or her blog site at www.gailmartin.blogspot.com. Write to Gail at P.O. Box 760063, Lathrup Village, MI, 48076, or at authorgailmartin@aol.com. She enjoys hearing from readers.

Books by Gail Gaymer Martin

Don't miss out on any of our super romances. Write to us at the following address for information on our newest releases and club information.

Heartsong Presents Readers' Service
PO Box 721
Uhrichsville, OH 44683

Or visit www.heartsongpresents.com

And Baby Makes Five

Gail Gaymer Martin

Heartsong Presents

Dedicated to my niece Andrea who lives in Salinas and provided me with great information.

Thanks also to my nephew Joe Fernandez for his medical information, and to Judy Rasmussen at Natividad Medical Center.

Thanks also to those who provided me with the help in the Spanish translations.

A note from the Author:
I love to hear from my readers! You may correspond with me by writing:

Gail Gaymer Martin
Author Relations
PO Box 721
Uhrichsville, OH 44683

ISBN 978-1-59789-638-2

AND BABY MAKES FIVE

All scripture quotations, unless otherwise indicated, are taken from the HOLY BIBLE, NEW INTERNATIONAL VERSION®. NIV®. Copyright © 1973, 1978, 1984 by International Bible Society. Used by permission of Zondervan. All rights reserved.

Our mission is to publish and distribute inspirational products offering exceptional value and biblical encouragement to the masses.

PRINTED IN THE U.S.A.

one

Felisa Carrillo's pain surged down her lower back into her belly. She doubled over in agony while the hot California sun beat across her back. She took deep breaths, controlling the spasms that weakened her knees, and struggled against falling to the lettuce field as the wave of pain raked through her.

"*¿Estás bien?*"

Her coworker's voice wrapped around her, but she couldn't answer. No, she wasn't okay, although Maria's tone alerted Felisa that she knew the answer to her question.

Maria boosted herself from her haunches, dropped the head of lettuce into the basket, and darted to her side. "*¿El bebé está naciendo?*"

When the pain subsided, Felisa lifted her head. "Yes, the baby is coming," she said in Spanish. She looked down the green, even rows to find a place to escape to, but instead her breath left her when she saw a man striding her way. The boss. The owner. She recognized him from other visits to his fields.

"*Déjeme ayudarte,*" Maria said, offering to help her. She slid her arm around Felisa's shoulder, trying to support her.

"*El jefe. El dueño.*" Panic filled Felisa, and she motioned toward the owner, warning Maria of his presence as she tried to pull away. "Maria, you must get back to work," she whispered in Spanish.

"No." Maria's voice snapped with determination.

Felisa slipped from her arms and knelt beside the lettuce, gesturing for her to leave.

Maria finally moved away and crouched farther down the

row while Felisa struggled to focus on a plant to avoid drawing the owner's attention. The earthy scent of sun-heated soil and foliage swept over her, causing her stomach to churn. She couldn't get sick now.

As she reached for a lettuce head, another contraction stabbed her. Panic filled her as the man moved closer. She couldn't afford to lose her job, and she sent up a prayer that God would help her bear the pain until he passed. She puffed to control the twisting anguish that seared inside her as the man's shadow fell across her and stopped.

"Are you ill?" His raspy voice hovered above her. "*¿Está usted enferma?*" he repeated.

She didn't look up but only shook her head.

He didn't move.

Tears ballooned in her eyes and escaped to her cheeks. She knew the droplets would leave a telltale trail on her dusty skin. She tried to brush them away, but she felt the sticky grime against her fist.

The man lowered his hand and tilted her face upward into the glaring sun. She flinched with his touch and closed her eyes to the brightness, but when she opened them she saw only concern in his eyes. His gaze left her face and lowered to her bulging belly she'd tried to camouflage with an oversized shirt. "Pregnant," he muttered then lifted his gaze to her face. "*¿Está usted embarazada?*"

She tugged at her top to cover her belly and ignored his question, but she felt her face go pale.

"You're in labor." His voice sounded disbelieving, and he bent over her as frustration rattled in his throat. He straightened and scanned the field. "Husband?" he muttered before he turned to her again. "*¿Dónde está su esposo?*"

Felisa's throat knotted. "Dead." *And good riddance,* she added to herself. She immediately became ashamed of her thought, but she knew God understood.

"You speak English." Relief filled his face.

"Yes."

"Your husband is dead?"

Felisa gave a fleeting nod. "Killed."

She watched his head swivel as he studied the field, like he were looking for a body. Finally he turned back to her, seemingly satisfied. "When? What happened?"

She winced, remembering the day she saw Miguel's mangled body. Though she knew some English, under stress she struggled to remember the words. "*Ocho*—eight months ago. *Accidente*—an accident," she corrected. Miguel had been drunk as always, but that day he was dead drunk. Coming out of a barroom, he staggered into the street and was hit by a car. The police called it an accident. She called it freedom.

The man shook his head and drew out a handkerchief to wipe the perspiration from his face. "Do you have family in Salinas?"

"No," she said, feeling another contraction grip her. She coiled into a ball.

"No family."

She heard the irritation in his voice.

"You're not having a baby in this field," he said, his voice deepening with emotion. "I'll take you to the hospital."

"No, please," she said, fearing a hospital bill. She barely had enough for food.

"The Natividad Medical Center. It's a hospital. You're not staying here," he said, sounding determined and hitting numbers on his cell phone. "Can you walk?"

He turned his attention to the phone call while she let the last of the pain fade. Could she walk? Determination charged through her. She would. She had to.

The man disconnected, then reached toward her.

"I can walk," she said, pushing her hand against the pungent earth to hoist herself. As she rose, her legs buckled, and he grasped her arm, lifting her to her feet and supporting her along the lettuce rows.

"My truck is this way." He motioned toward the distance.

Felisa felt her knees buckle again, and she stumbled forward. The man scooped her into his arms and carried her, his urgency obvious. His strength gave her a sense of security, and she drew in the smell of the heat radiating from his skin, a clean aroma so different from the workers in the field. His fresh scent mingled with the tangy fragrance of his aftershave.

"Do you think you can make it?" he asked. "By the time I get an ambulance here, we can probably be there." He boosted her more securely against his body.

A wave of pain bore down on her, and she struggled until she could speak. "I'll make it." Yet her voice sounded breathless and insecure. She recoiled with anger at her stupid response. She had no idea if she could make it. What if he had to deliver the baby? As she opened her mouth to retract her statement, Felisa felt the man shift her weight and realized they'd reached his truck.

"Can you stand?" he asked as he lowered his arms.

She nodded, and he braced her against him as he pulled out his keys, then opened the door and lifted her onto the seat. "We'll be there in a few minutes." He eyed her again. "Are you sure you can do this?"

She had little choice. "I'm okay," she answered, praying that God would keep the baby safe until she reached the clinic.

He closed the door, and in a moment the driver's side door opened and he slipped in beside her. The ignition kicked in, and she leaned her head against the leathery seat cushion as the truck bumped and rocked when they pulled away. Her gaze rested on his tanned hands gripping the steering wheel, and she saw concern in his bearing.

A cool breeze washed over her legs—air-conditioning, a luxury she and her husband had never been able to afford. She felt blessed her junker car still ran. Sometimes it was not only her transportation but also her bed, more often than she wanted to remember, and now with the baby what would she—

"What's your name?"

His voice jerked her from her thoughts. She eyed his profile. "Felisa Carrillo."

"And you have no family here?"

"None. My parents live near Guadalajara."

"You should go back home."

His blunt comment punctured her. "I can't."

He glanced at her, his hazel eyes flashing a questioning look, but he didn't probe further.

A sudden fear settled over Felisa. What did he want of her? Why had he insisted on taking her to the hospital when so many women had their babies in the fields or outbuildings, anyplace they could find privacy and cover?

She tilted her head to search his face. Determination had settled in his jaw, his lips pressed together, and his hands gripped the wheel with purpose. Would he try to take her child away from her? Would he offer to buy her baby? She'd heard stories of people bargaining for the migrants' children, and they were so poor they would give in to their weakness. She would not, but she had no money to fight a battle, no money to—

Another contraction wracked her, and Felisa bit her lip to keep from screaming. She focused on the cool air of the cab and the soft hum of the engine, letting the pain seep away until she could breathe. She didn't even know the man's name. They'd all referred to him as el dueño, the owner. That was all she knew.

"I'm Chad Garrison," he said as if hearing her thoughts. "I own the farm."

"I know." She brushed her gritty fingers through her hair that matted against her cheek.

"What would you have done if I hadn't come along?"

"I—I. . ." Giving birth in the field was nothing new; yet how could she tell him she would have done what other women had to do?

"You would have had the baby in the field. Do you realize that?"

"Yes," she whispered, wishing she'd had a better plan, but being without a husband, she had no other means.

"Unbelievable," he said, shaking his head as if disgusted. "Don't you realize the danger? How could you think that little of bringing a life into the world?"

Felisa felt dirty and worthless. "I know." Even his shiny new truck seemed more worthy than she felt. She felt more like her old car, which had lost its sheen just as her life had lost its color.

His neck twisted with the speed of a bullet, and his eyes narrowed. She felt like a flyspeck beneath his gaze until his look softened. "I'm sorry. I don't mean to judge you. I suppose you have little choice."

The expression in his eyes broke her heart, as if the danger she was in belonged to him. She studied his face again, his firm chin and lips so full they looked soft and pliable when earlier they had looked rigid and compressed. Felisa didn't respond to his comment. She had nothing to say. She'd made her decisions and married badly. Her life had become one sleazy motel or low-income housing unit after another, and since Miguel's death, it had been even worse. She closed her eyes as the next sudden pain nearly rent her in two.

৯৹

Chad pulled his hand away from the steering wheel and

stretched his cramped fingers. He'd gripped the wheel as though he feared for his life. Emptiness hammered in his chest. He glanced at the young Hispanic woman beside him, sorry he'd lost control and snapped at her. Her presence triggered horrific memories that tore through him—memories he'd kept deep inside for the past two years.

Felisa's dark hair clung in ringlets against her damp face. He longed to brush it back to make her more comfortable. Instead he adjusted the air conditioner, but reality told him it was the pain that caused her to perspire and not the heat. The bright rays came through the window and shone through her dark tresses glinting with streaks of copper, as if they had been bleached by the sun.

He watched a grimace surge across Felisa's face. Another contraction. Chad looked ahead, praying they reached the medical center before the baby came. He'd been foolish not to call for an ambulance; but he figured by the time they arrived it would be too late and the baby would be born in the field. Even cattle had the comfort of hay in the shelter of a barn. This woman deserved that much. The thought of the Christmas story charged through his mind, when Mary birthed Jesus in the covering of a stall.

He watched the speed limit as he hurried down Natividad Road, and when he crossed Laurel Drive, Chad drew in a lengthy breath. Only a few more yards and he could put the young woman into the hands of the medical staff. "We're almost there," he said, hearing relief in his voice.

He took the emergency entrance and pulled up to the door as a medic met him with a wheelchair. Chad jumped from the truck and hurried around to the passenger side where the medic was already helping the woman into the chair.

"Good thing you called. Looks like you got her here just in time," the man said as he lowered the footrest while Felisa raised her feet to the platform. He released the brake and headed inside.

Chad stood for a moment, watching her until she vanished through the doorway. He drew in a breath, turned, and climbed into the truck. He sat for a few seconds, deciding what was right. Chad had nothing to do with this woman and had done his duty. He could leave.

He turned on the ignition and pulled away from the emergency door, but his conscience prickled in his thoughts. She was his employee. What if she ran into a problem? Would she be all right? Would the baby make it through the ordeal? Chad figured Felisa had received no prenatal care. He'd seen that before, and it knotted in his chest.

Chad knew what the Lord would have him do. He turned the wheel and pulled into a parking slot, then climbed out and strode toward the entrance. He could at least make sure someone had taken care of her.

The summer heat beat against his shoulders as his boots clicked along the concrete walk. Chad passed the security guard with a nod as the double door swished open. Inside he was greeted with air-conditioning and the scent of antiseptic. He strode to the desk and waited until the woman raised her head. "I just brought in Felisa—" Felisa what? He'd already forgotten her last name. "She's in labor. A young Hispan—"

"She's in the back," she said. "You're her husband?"

Her question yanked at his memory. "She's my employee. She has no family here."

"You can wait in the visitor area." She swung her arm toward the hallway. "Mrs. Carrillo is in delivery."

Chad glanced at his watch, remembering the list of jobs he was supposed to do today. "How long will it be?"

She rolled her eyes and shook her head. "Babies come in their own time, sir."

"I realize that." He lowered his head and backed away, irritated with himself and with her. He paused, then turned toward the door, deciding to forget his attempt to be a good Samaritan.

"Sir."

He halted and pivoted toward her.

"Let me call delivery and see how she's doing."

"Thank you." He shoved his hands into his pockets and stepped forward.

She nodded and picked up the telephone while he waited. His mind tumbled with painful memories. Only two years ago he'd waited like this at Salinas Valley Memorial Hospital—the horrible long wait with a horrendous ending.

"She's delivering now, sir. It won't be long."

Her voice pushed its way into Chad's consciousness. "Now?"

"You apparently got here just in time." She motioned again to the waiting room. "Why not wait a few minutes? The doctor will see you shortly."

His mind reeling with memories, Chad forced himself to focus on today. He turned and made his way to the waiting room. Inside, he stopped to pour a cup of strong black coffee from the carafe. Its acrid scent permeated the room. He crumpled into a nearby chair and leaned back his head, wondering how he'd gotten into the mess in the first place. Chad glanced at his watch again, then pulled out his cell phone, punched in the numbers, and waited for an answer.

"Joe," he said, once he connected, "I'm at—" He stopped himself. "I'm on an errand and can't get back for a while. Can you handle things until I get there?"

As he expected, Joe had no problem with his request and didn't ask what was keeping him. He didn't want to lie, but he didn't want to tell the truth. He'd avoided getting familiar with his workers. Their plight ate at his conscience. So many lived in less-than-acceptable housing with little to offer their families, but migratory workers were the backbone of his business. He paid them better than most did and tried to provide temporary housing, although the task was endless and often hopeless.

He closed his eyes, envisioning the lovely young woman now facing a dilemma. How could she work with a new baby? Where would she go? His fingers knotted into fists against the vinyl upholstery. He felt responsible for some reason, angry at the whole situation—her husband dying, her pregnancy, the fact that his own visit to the field this morning had brought her into his life. He could have gone anywhere but that field.

He opened his eyes, his thoughts filled with shame. Where was his compassion? His upbringing? *Lord, You have the answers. I'll put my trust in You. I can't solve these never-ending problems. I place this in Your hands.*

He rose and poured the coffee down the drain, then tucked his hands into his pockets and paced. When he met the eyes of other families waiting, they smiled as if understanding his anxiety, but they didn't understand. He wasn't the father. He shouldn't be involved, but he'd gotten himself into it.

Chad strode to the window and looked out at the beaming sun in the clear blue sky. He wished Felisa's future could be as bright as the heavens.

"Mr. Carrillo?"

Awareness clicked in Chad. *Carrillo.* That was Felisa's last name. He turned to see a physician in green scrubs, a mask dangling around his neck. Heat rose up Chad's face. He pulled his hands from his pockets and strode toward the physician, his hand extended.

The doctor gripped his fingers. "Congratulations! You're the father—"

"I'm not the father."

The physician's eyes widened.

"She's a widow and works for me. I brought her in."

The doctor's handshake loosened, and he stepped back. "She and the baby are fine."

Discomfort settled on Chad's shoulders. "Boy or girl?"

"A boy."

A boy. Chad thought of his twin daughters so lost without their mother, who died delivering Chad's stillborn baby son. The pain seared through his chest. "I'm glad they're okay," he said finally, monitoring the emotion that welled inside him.

"You can see them if you'd like. It will be a few minutes."

"No, I—" *I what? I'm a wimp?* Chad swallowed, hoping to regain his control. "I'd like to see the boy."

"I'll send a nurse in when he's ready."

The doctor backed away, and Chad turned and settled into the chair he'd occupied earlier. A boy. A new life. And what a life the small infant had to face. Reality pressed down upon him like a lead weight as a prayer rose to heaven, begging the Lord to care for this woman and child.

Time dragged, and Chad had second thoughts. He should leave. He'd done his duty as a Christian. He knew she was in good hands for now. Slipping his hand into his pocket, he felt the car keys jingle against his fingers. He wrapped his fist around the keys and pulled them upward.

"Is someone waiting to see the Carrillo baby?"

Chad's head swiveled toward the nurse in the doorway. He didn't have to answer, but his mouth opened. "Yes. Thank you."

He met her in the hallway and followed her down a corridor. Realizing they weren't heading to a nursery, he faltered.

"Is something wrong?"

"No, but I thought—"

"Wait a minute." She held up one finger. "I'll check inside." She strode into the room and came out again. "Mrs. Carrillo is sleeping, but you can see the baby."

His heartbeat slowed. Felisa was sleeping. His throat knotted. It wasn't his place to look at her child, and he couldn't talk to Felisa now; but he wanted to see the boy.

The nurse gave him a questioning look, and he pulled himself together and followed her, his mind swinging from one direction to another. They passed the first bed, then stepped around a curtain. His heart jumped when he saw Felisa, her eyelids closed, her breathing soft. She looked tired, yet beautiful. He forced his attention toward the nurse standing beside a bassinet.

"I'll leave you alone," she said and left the room.

Chad lowered his gaze. He looked into the tiny face of Felisa's beautiful baby with dark, curling hair and creamy bronzed skin. His chest ached as he studied the tiny fingers and black lashes that flickered beneath the bright light.

"Welcome to the world, little boy," he said. "Welcome to harsh reality." He felt the car keys still gripped in his fingers and wished he'd fled instead of seeing this helpless babe who needed so much love and security.

He tore his gaze away and turned his back to the room. Sadness washed over him, and he hurried down the hallway and out into the sunny day. Sunny for him, but not sunny for that beautiful little boy.

two

Felisa cradled her son in her arms. Tears of joy rolled down her cheeks until reality set in. What did she have to offer this child God had given her? She worked hard yet got nowhere. She couldn't return to her parents' house in Guadalajara. They had rejoiced each time one of the seven children had left the nest, making one less mouth to feed. They were as bad off as she was. Worse, maybe. She couldn't burden them now with her problem.

She gazed down at her beautiful child and tucked her finger into the baby's palm, feeling his tiny fist curl around it—perfect little fingers, bronzy and soft, a tiny life that had lived inside her during the worst of times. He would grow up to be strong, and, God willing, maybe he would have a better life than she had. Felisa drew in a deep breath, determined her son would succeed where she'd failed. But how? It seemed so hopeless.

She promised herself this boy would never be like his father. Never. She closed her eyes, knowing she couldn't make such a promise. She had no power to make things better. Only God could guide her son's destiny. She bowed her head, asking God to bless her baby and keep him strong in body and faith. Her faith had been what she'd clung to the past year, a faith that had been strengthened by a wise Christian woman who'd taken her under her wing and taught her more about Jesus. She would be grateful forever, because her faith now burned in her heart more brightly.

A sound outside her room caught her attention. Her heart

fluttered as she wondered if she had company. Chad Garrison's powerful image filled her mind, but when she looked toward the doorway, an aide entered the room, pushing a cart with carafes of fresh water. Felisa drew up her shoulders and smiled at her son. "We don't need anyone," she whispered. "It's you and me. . .and the heavenly Father. That's all we need."

You and me. Felisa Carrillo and who? She studied the baby's face, his tiny nose and the dark eyelashes that brushed against his soft cheeks. Tears welled in her eyes. *What is your name?* God had written her child's name in the book of life. A deep ache burned in her, wondering what life held in store for her little boy.

She watched the aide straighten her bed table and replace the water, then slip from the room without a word. She lowered her gaze to the tiny features, the soft cuddly form that lay against her body. "You are my son," she whispered. "Only mine. By what name will you be called?" She searched through the list of family names, men she worked beside, but nothing seemed to stir her heart.

In the quiet her thoughts again turned to Chad Garrison. Why had he been so kind? Rarely did the workers ever see the farm owner in the fields. The field managers told the workers what to do and saw that they did it. Had this man acted out of kindness or for some ulterior motive? The thought frightened her.

Her earlier horrible questions returned. Would he allow her to continue to work at his farm without giving him her son? It might be for the best, but she couldn't give away her child. Her mind swirled with fears; yet in her heart she wanted to think he was only being kind. A knot of confusion coiled in her chest and rose to her throat. "Dearest Lord, take care of us," she whispered as tears pooled in her eyes and ran down her cheeks.

❧

Chad looked up from his desk in the field office and saw Joe standing in the doorway.

"So you're back," Joe said, ambling into the room and slumping into a chair.

He cocked his head, hoping to avoid the foreman's questions. He spread his arms, managing a grin. "Looks like it, doesn't it? Here I am."

Joe leaned forward and folded his hands between his knees. "Heard you helped a woman off the field this morning."

"You did, huh?" He kept his eyes focused on his work.

"Right. What's up?"

Chad dropped his pen onto his untidy blotter and leaned back. "You tell me. Sounds like someone already told you the story."

"Mexican woman in labor. That's what I heard."

"Then you heard right."

Joe leaned even closer, questions written on his face.

Trying to avoid eye contact, Chad stared at the ledger, then picked up the pen; yet he feared the interrogation wasn't over.

"And?" Joe's voice punctuated the silence.

Chad tossed the pen onto the desk again. "What do you want to know?"

Joe shrugged. "I don't know. What happened? You've never done that before."

"I've never watched a woman nearly give birth in the field before. I took her to Natividad Medical Center. What did you expect me to do?"

Joe rose from the chair. "Don't bite my head off. I was just curious."

"Curiosity killed the cat."

Joe raised his arms in a hopeless gesture and strode toward the door.

"I'm sorry," Chad said, watching Joe brace his hands against the doorframe for a moment, then turn to face him.

"What's gotten into you, Chad? It's not like you—"

"I know." His head lowered, and he wove through the millions of feelings churning inside him. He regained composure and looked at Joe. "I saw the woman in labor, and I couldn't help but think of—"

"Janie." Joe looked stunned and moved toward him from the doorway, his expression filled with sympathy. "I'm sorry, man. I didn't think. It makes sense that you'd think of your wife." He settled back into the chair. "You did the right thing."

Chad wondered. Now that he'd become tangled in this woman's problem, he couldn't let it go. Distraction followed him home from the hospital while his thoughts drifted again to Felisa's needs. Felisa. He'd never bothered to learn the names of his workers. It made them too real, and now this woman and her baby were too real. "She had a boy."

Joe didn't respond but looked at him, his eyes searching Chad's face as if wondering what he'd gotten himself into.

He felt defensive with Joe's probing look. "I didn't go in to see the woman."

Joe let out a stream of breath as if relieved. "Don't get too involved, Chad. It's a hopeless situation."

Chad heaved back his chair, hearing the scrape of the legs against the wooden floor, and rose, his chest tightening with Joe's reality. "I know. I know, but—"

"You did your good deed. Natividad will take the financial loss, and you can feel good you did that much."

That much. The woman could survive, but that baby boy. What about him?

Joe didn't move, and Chad felt his inquisitive stare.

"Don't you have work to do?" Chad asked, sending an arched brow his way.

"Sure I do. I just thought. . ." He let the rest of his sentence die as he headed for the door.

Chad waited until he heard the click, then collapsed into the chair and lowered his face in his hands. He knew it wasn't wise, but he had to make sure this woman had a place to go. The hospital wouldn't keep her more than a day or so—just long enough to make sure they were healthy. She'd be sent out to face the world, but not alone. This time with a child. He cringed, knowing what he had to do and knowing he would be sorry.

&

Night would soon settle over the city, and Felisa could see streaks of dusky rose spreading across the sky from the setting sun. Soon the city lights would come alive like fireflies at her window. She nestled deeper under the blankets, unaccustomed to air-conditioning—such a luxury. Felisa imagined her friends fanning themselves against the heat before the sun vanished and the cooler air drifted into the valley.

She closed her eyes and worried about tomorrow. If she was released, where would she go? She'd missed a day's work and probably two, she guessed. Her pay would be so little, and now she needed things for the baby.

She pictured her child's sweet face, longing to know what he would look like grown up. His father had been a handsome man. That had been her foolish downfall. She should have listened to her friends' warnings, but she'd been so certain, and she never asked the Lord to help her make a godly decision. She'd tripped over her wisdom to marry Miguel. She'd been so young. Sixteen. Felisa hardly knew what marriage was to be, although she'd seen her parents' struggle. Why hadn't she been smart enough to realize what life would hold for her?

Footsteps caught her attention, and when the privacy curtain drew back, her heart skipped a beat. Chad Garrison stepped inside and stopped at the foot of her bed, silent as a stone.

Felisa pushed her hair away from her face, knowing she must look a fright. She had nothing with her to make herself look better. She hadn't even combed her hair that she could remember. Felisa lowered her gaze, unable to look him in the eye. Questions filled her mind. Why was he there? What did he want of her? Panic knotted in her chest.

"How are you?" he asked, his voice raspy but gentle.

"Fine," she said.

She sensed he'd stepped closer and heard the chair shift on the tile floor before he sat beside her hospital bed. "Your boy is a handsome baby."

Her arms wrenched against her chest, wanting to hold her child in her arms, to protect him. She would not give him away—not for any money on earth. "Thank you," she mumbled.

Despite her attempt to cover her fear, her voice sounded cautious. He must have sensed her concern, because he leaned closer and said her name.

Felisa lifted her gaze, afraid of what she'd see, but again she saw only kindness in his soft hazel eyes.

"I want to ask you a few questions. I know this isn't my business, really. You're only an employee. That's it, and all you owe me is a good day's work. But I brought you here, and now I feel. . ."

His voice drifted off, and she studied his face, wondering what he felt. Surely he didn't feel he owed her anything. No other employer had ever provided anything beyond her wage.

His mouth tensed. "I'm concerned about your working in the field with the baby."

"I'm fine. Look at him." She motioned toward the bassinet. "My son's fine. I can work." She felt tears blur her vision.

He couldn't fire her. She had no money and nowhere to go. She had—

"I'm not doubting you can work, but you have the baby." He rose and looked at her boy a moment before turning back to her. "Do you have someone to care for him? Where are you living?"

"I have help. Don't worry." She didn't have any earthly help, but she knew where her help came from. A voice rose in her mind. *"My help comes from the Lord."*

"Felisa, where do you live?"

His voice sounded stern, and she lowered her gaze. What could she say that wasn't a lie? "I make out okay."

"That's not what I asked you. It's not just you, but your child. I want to know if you have a home. Are you in the government housing?"

Although she sensed concern in his voice, she didn't want to let down her guard. "No, but I can make do."

"Then where—"

"I rent a motel room," she said then realized she had to tell him the whole truth. "When I can afford one."

"If not, do you stay with someone?"

"I'll ask around. Maybe—"

"You don't sleep in the train or bus station, do you?"

She shook her head, although she knew those who did. "My car. I own a car."

"You live out of your car?"

"Sometimes, but—"

He rose and jammed his hands into his pockets. "I'll make some calls. Do you know when you'll be released?"

"Why?" The question flew from her mouth.

"Why?" He looked confused. "I want to know when you're released so I can—"

"No, not that. Why are you helping me? What do you want?"

He drew back as if she'd slapped him. "I don't want anything. You have a child, and you need a home for the baby."

She eyed him, her suspicion raging. "No one has ever offered me anything. I don't understand."

He shook his head. "You don't need to understand."

But she did. "I don't want to lose my son."

"I don't want you to, either, and you won't. I'll ask at the desk, and I'll talk with you tomorrow."

He turned and stepped toward the curtain; but it opened, and a nurse entered the room pushing a monitor. "Time for your blood pressure," she said. "Do you want to sit up?"

"In a minute," she said, eyeing her employer and wondering if he were leaving.

He didn't move away. Instead he shifted closer to the bassinet and looked down at her child. A mixture of fear and pride waged war inside her. She studied him as he bent lower as if to touch her son.

"Do you mind?" he asked, looking at Felisa over his shoulder.

"No." But she wasn't sure if she minded or not. He'd said kind things to her, but did he mean them?

He brushed the baby's cheek with his finger and smiled.

"Would you like to hold him?" Felisa asked, startled when the words left her.

He glanced from her to the nurse with a questioning look on his face.

"Have a seat," the nurse said, pointing to the chair he'd just vacated.

He sank into the chair, and Felisa wondered if he'd had second thoughts about whether he wanted to hold the baby, but he didn't have time to decline. The nurse lifted the infant from the bassinet and nestled him into Chad's arms, then moved back to Felisa with the blood pressure cuff.

Felisa watched his face flicker with deep emotion. Her pulse tripped, wondering what thoughts were running through his head. She'd thought he had evil on his mind; yet now she sensed something deep and sad stirring inside him, something she would never know, but whatever it was it gave Felisa a feeling of confidence in him. Maybe he was a good man who really wanted to help her.

Chad sat for a moment and watched the nurse pump up the cuff and listen through her stethoscope; then he glanced at Felisa with a mournful smile, holding her son in stiff arms as if he feared he might break.

"You didn't have to hold him," she said, concerned about his discomfort.

"It's fine." He seemed to relax and study the baby again. "He's a good-looking boy already. I think he has your chin and the same large eyes as yours."

Her chin. Her eyes. She had no idea he'd even really looked at her. "Thank you. I pray he's kind and honest. Good looks aren't as important." Miguel burst into her mind, and she wished she'd realized that seven years ago, before she married him.

"That's it," the nurse said, unwrapping the cuff from her arm. "Everything looks good." She grasped the monitor and pushed it past the curtain.

Chad had turned his attention back to the baby. "What's his name?"

Felisa scooted to the edge of the bed and looked over at her sleeping son. "I haven't decided." She looked into Chad's eyes and again saw that faraway look.

"A boy needs a name," Chad said. "Something special for this one."

Something special. Her baby was special. He was her family, part of her being. Felisa's thoughts drifted to her family in

Guadalajara, and she was filled with melancholy. "My mother once told me she would have named me Nataniel if I'd been a boy."

"That's a nice name."

"It means gift from God."

Chad lifted his gaze to hers, and her heart flooded with warmth as he brushed his thick finger over the baby's cheek.

"I've decided to name my son Nataniel," she said, feeling more relaxed in her employer's company, "and call him Nate."

"That's a good name. A very good choice." He leaned over the baby. "Welcome to the world, Nataniel."

"Nate," she whispered.

"Nate it is." He rose and settled the baby into her arms. "I need to make some calls. I'll talk with you tomorrow, and I hope you'll have a place to stay."

"Thank you," she said, admiring his tall, lanky frame as he strode across the room.

He gave her a fleeting look and slipped behind the curtain.

Felisa looked down at her son. She pictured her baby in Chad Garrison's arms, and she prayed her instinct about the man had been right. He seemed to be a sensitive person—a kind man. She hoped he wanted only to help her and Nate. Hearing her son's name in her thoughts sent shivers of joy through her. Her child deserved better than she could offer, and if this man could help, she would accept his offer. Just this once.

≈

The morning sunlight flickered beneath the blinds of Chad's Corral de Tierra home. He stirred under the sheet and opened one eye to gaze at the alarm clock. Six thirty. He hadn't rested well last night, his mind shifting from Felisa's dilemma to his own emotions, which had been rattled since he'd driven the woman to the hospital.

He yawned but couldn't indulge his desire to sleep. He had work to do. On the way out of the hospital last evening, he'd asked at the desk about Felisa's release. Though they were unsure without a doctor's statement, the nurse calculated today or tomorrow at the latest. The baby and Felisa were both healthy, and without insurance they wouldn't keep the mother and child in the hospital too long, he knew.

Chad shifted his feet from beneath the covering and sat on the edge of the bed. He ran his fingers through his hair, thinking about where to begin. The first thing to do was call the agency regarding housing facilities, units used for migrant workers. The cost was low, and the government facilities always provided daycare. Still with over 250,000 farm workers in need of housing each year, he knew he couldn't take availability for granted. He could only hope.

After rising, Chad showered, shaved, and headed to the kitchen. The scent of coffee and the fragrant aroma of cinnamon beckoned him down the hallway. He came around the corner in time to see his housekeeper pull a tray of pastries from the oven.

"Good morning," she said, setting the tray on a rack. "You're just in time."

"Thanks, Juanita," he said, grasping a cup from the rack and filling it with steaming black coffee. He settled onto a kitchen chair, took a cautious sip of the drink, and flipped open his cell phone. He flicked through the address book for the Office of Migrant Services and hit the call button. OMS worked hard to provide inexpensive housing for the vast number of workers who streamed into the area during planting and harvest. He sent up a prayer that they would have housing for Felisa and the baby. Now he could only hope someone was there this early.

Juanita set a plate in front of him with a warm cinnamon

pastry and slices of fresh fruit. She walked away, and he heard her hit the toaster button.

"This is enough for today, Juanita," he said, gesturing to the dish in front of him. His stomach felt knotted with his thoughts. When his call connected, he listened to the automated menu list, irritated that finding a human at the end of the line seemed impossible. Finally he hit the zero, and his shoulders relaxed when a human voice responded. "Is Bill Garcia available? This is Chad Garrison of Garrison Farms."

He waited, listening to music strum over the lines, until he heard a hello. "Bill, this is Chad Garrison. I have a favor. I need housing for one of my workers. She just gave birth to a baby at Natividad and should be released either—"

Bill's voice cut into his explanation, and Chad shrank with his abrupt response.

"Nothing? She only needs a small place. She's desperate."

Bill's voice sounded weary, and Chad thought about the time. The guy had probably come in early to catch up on paperwork.

"I see," Chad said. "What about another facility not too far from Salinas? Do you know if—"

Bill's answer snapped through the speaker.

"Nothing. You're sure?" He listened to Bill's comments. He'd heard the story before. The waiting list and the tenant council who worked to fill available spaces. "Thanks anyway, Bill. I'll have to give this some thought."

He closed the cell phone with a flip and set it on the table, discouragement coursing through him. What now? Most low-cost motels were filled, he knew, and even then, what would Felisa do with the baby while she worked? Chad couldn't imagine her bringing the newborn in a baby backpack while trying to pick lettuce. Yet he'd seen that done, too.

Juanita hovered nearby, cleaning the counter from her

baking and readying things to pack Chad's lunch. Since he'd hired her she'd been a wonderful, hardworking woman, and she'd put up with the antics of his twins uncomplainingly.

"Are the girls up yet?" Chad asked.

"No. Nanny said she'd hog-tie them if they got up too early. She's losing patience, I'm afraid, just like the others."

Juanita surprised him. She had never been one to gossip, so her comment made an impact on him. He'd noticed the nanny hadn't been the most patient woman. Yet his four-year-olds could try most anyone's patience. He had to bite his tongue many times to keep from yelling at them himself. The words in Proverbs had entered his mind more than once. *A gentle answer turns away wrath, but a harsh word stirs up anger.* He'd tried to follow God's direction, but he'd nearly failed many times.

"Juanita, you know the area. I'm looking for housing for one of my workers who—"

"I couldn't help but hear you," she said, stopping her work. "I don't know anyplace that has openings. Where has she been living, and what about her husband?"

Her question aroused his emotion. "She's a young widow. From what she told me, her husband died only a month after she conceived. I'm guessing she's been sleeping in her car somewhere."

Juanita shook her head and took a deep breath. "Very sad. Such a difficult life. I'm grateful to my parents that they worked hard and made a good life for us. I'm able to fend for myself."

"You've been blessed, Juanita."

"I can ask around and see if any of the housekeepers in the area know if their employers are looking for help, but I think that's a lost cause." She paused and then gave him an uncomfortable look. "Is she trustworthy?"

He shook his head. "I don't know the woman, but I'd guess she is."

Juanita shrugged. "I'll ask around when I finish up here."

"She'll be released today or tomorrow. That doesn't give much time."

"I'll do my best," she said, opening the refrigerator door.

He studied Juanita. She'd been a faithful employee and worked hard, almost too hard, and never complained. He admired her for that. She deserved a break.

three

Chad stood outside Felisa's hospital room the next afternoon, amazed. He had sensed the Lord leading him to help her, but he felt overwhelmed by the Lord's request. He felt drawn to her and her needs; yet it set him on edge. People had attitudes. People talked. Joe's criticism came to mind.

Earlier in the day Felisa had called, and he could still hear her tentative voice. She'd called his home first, and Juanita had provided his cell phone number. When he'd answered he'd hoped the call would be good news about housing. Instead it was her soft request. "Can you pick me up? I have no way to get to my car."

Get to my car. Her words pierced his heart, and he'd made his decision at that moment.

He drew in a deep breath and walked through the door into her room. He gave a nod to the patient in the first bed, then stood outside the curtain. "Are you dressed?" he asked.

"I'm ready," she said, her voice as gentle as a breeze rippling the colorful bougainvillea blossoms outside.

He slid the curtain over and stepped inside. Felisa sat on the edge of the bed, dressed in the same clothing he'd brought her in with. What did he expect? Who would bring her clean clothes?

She turned to look at him over her shoulder. "Thank you for coming." Her face looked pale, with worry lines on her forehead.

He walked farther into the room and leaned over the bassinet to look at the tiny boy. Nate. He had a name. Chad's chest tightened, and he forced himself away, trying to repress the memories that flooded his mind. "Do you need to do anything before you leave?" He sat in the same chair he'd used to hold the baby the day before.

She shook her head, then thought better. "I have to wait for a wheelchair."

He motioned toward the call button. "Let's buzz the nurse and tell her you're ready."

Felisa leaned over and signaled the nurse's station. When she finished she rose and straightened her oversized top. "I'm sorry. I don't have any clean clothes with me."

"I should have asked if you needed anything," he said, wondering where she kept her belongings. In her car, he guessed.

She looked pale and frightened, and she wandered to the window, looking out, then turned, walked past the curtain, and peered toward the corridor.

"It'll be a while, Felisa. You might as well sit."

She stopped pacing, looking as jittery as he felt, and he wondered how she would react when she learned he hadn't found a room as he'd promised.

Felisa sank onto the edge of the bed and gazed toward the window. He wondered what she thought of him. She'd already mentioned that no one had ever treated her so well. Chad wondered if she needed his reassurance. He sensed she was looking for his motive. The more he thought about it, the more he knew he needed to say something.

"I've tried to help you, Felisa, but I expect nothing in return. I don't want you to worry that I had any motive other than to help a fellow human being. The Bible says what we do for others we do for Him, and I've tried to live my life that way."

Surprise registered on her face. "You're a Christian?" Her eyes searched his.

"I sure am."

He saw her shoulders relax and realized his comment had given her relief. "Did you think I had some other reason?"

She shrugged. "I didn't know. People—people sometimes want—want babies, and I—"

"No. No. I would never have—" He couldn't believe what she'd thought. "Did you really think I wanted to take your son from you?"

"I—I didn't know, but I couldn't imagine what you wanted from me, except. . ."

Her voice faded, and he could only guess the dire thoughts that had filled her mind.

"You have an unusual circumstance without a husband and now a new baby. I wanted to help you. I have two daughters of my own."

"Daughters?" Her dark eyes widened, and he saw a glint of interest that brightened her tense face.

"Two four-year-old girls. They're two handfuls. Maybe four handfuls." He chuckled, although it wasn't always a laughing matter.

Her gaze traveled over his face. "I'm sure they are beautiful children."

"They look like their mother did."

Her face twisted in question. "She is gone away?"

His chest constricted, taking away his breath. "In heaven. Maybe she knows your husband," he added, to make her aware he understood her sorrow.

"No." Her voice darkened. "Miguel is not in heaven. He didn't love Jesus, and he didn't follow His ways."

"You never know, Felisa," he said, sorry he'd mentioned her husband. He wondered if the man's faith was one of the deep regrets he saw in Felisa's eyes.

"I do know," she said. "Miguel will not be in heaven."

Awareness shot through Chad. Miguel had not been a good husband, he guessed. His sadness multiplied. The man had apparently led her into a world of migratory work, then stranded her there by dying. Chad couldn't believe Felisa would choose such a life. She'd mentioned her husband had died in an accident. Her comment made him curious.

The curtain shifted, and a volunteer appeared pushing a wheelchair. "Ready to go home?"

Felisa gave Chad a frantic look and nodded.

His heart ached for her. He glanced around the room, looking for something to carry while the attendant settled her in the chair and then handed her the baby. He saw nothing. No flowers, no luggage, no cards or gifts. Her aloneness made him weak.

As he followed the volunteer along the hallway, the woman paused at the desk and accepted a package. "This is for you and the baby."

Chad took the bag of gifts and mumbled a thank-you as they left. He glanced inside the plastic shopping bag and saw a bundle of diapers, items wrapped in paper and plastic, nothing that concerned him, and yet it did. He'd acted on compassion, and he would not stop now.

When they reached the outside door, Chad paused. "I'll bring the car up for you. Wait here." He took the plastic bag and headed through the door.

❧

"Is this your first child?" the volunteer asked, gazing down at Nate.

"Yes," Felisa said, thinking, *My first and last.* She couldn't raise children living in this environment, and she had no means to get out of it. She'd dropped out of school. She had no training other than housework. She'd always helped at home, and she could cook, but had no way to earn a real living.

The volunteer stood behind her, humming a nonsensical tune to pass the time, and Felisa was glad she'd stopped asking questions. She had no answers, and questions would only remind her she would now face the most trying time of her life.

Felisa looked toward the parking lot. She'd hoped her employer would be true to his word, but he hadn't mentioned finding her a place to live. She would have to make do in her car, or maybe she could ask Maria or another worker to take her in until the baby was a couple of months old.

Her head drooped as she faced the truth. She would never ask. Her coworkers were already in overcrowded conditions, and some were worse off than she with no car to call their own. Her pulse tripped when a sleek, deep blue car pulled up to the front door and Chad climbed out. He headed her way and propped the door open while the volunteer rolled her to the car.

"Where's your pickup?" Felisa asked, handing Nate to the volunteer while she rose from the wheelchair.

"Home," he said. Instead of opening the passenger door, he unlatched the back door and set the plastic bag inside.

Felisa felt her jaw drop. A newborn infant seat had been attached to the middle cushion. She stared at it, not knowing what to say. "This was your daughters'?"

"No," he said, "but you can't take Nate onto the highway without one." He gave her a warm smile. "Federally approved."

She couldn't help but smile at his playful expression. Felisa thanked the volunteer and took Nate into her arms. She followed Chad's direction and settled Nate into the seat, facing backward. She smiled at her son, so small and beautiful. He'd been the best little boy. He cried only when he was hungry, and then only a whimper.

"This seat is great," Chad said. "We didn't have this kind

for the twins. You don't have to remove the whole thing. See?" He pointed to the base of the infant seat with its special locks. "This part is stationary, and the top comes off as a baby carrier."

With Nate safely settled, Felisa slid into the car while Chad held the door.

"The salesman said this is the most secure seat," he added. "And if the baby's sleeping, he can stay in the carrier without waking up." He closed her door, and she watched him hurry around to the driver's side and open the door. "Another feature is the carrier fits into a stroller with a simple click."

She nearly chuckled at his excitement about the baby carrier until it registered concern. Why had he purchased a new car seat for Nate?

Chad smiled and settled beside her then turned the key in the ignition. "Here we go," he said, shifting into gear and rolling to the driveway.

"I can't thank you enough," she said, trying to squelch her fear. She twisted in her seatbelt to look behind her at the infant seat. "I don't know how I can pay you. I'd hoped to borrow—"

"I don't expect payment, Felisa. You'll need lots of things. A baby is expensive."

She felt her back stiffen. She didn't like charity, and she didn't want to be beholden to anyone. She owed him too much already. "I have things in my car that people gave me. I'll get by."

"In your car?" he said, a look of discomfort on his face.

She sensed she'd hurt his feelings with her comment. "I didn't have a car seat for Nate. I didn't think of that."

"Now you have one," he said. "It's a gift from me."

She mumbled a thank-you and looked out the passenger window, amazed she was riding in this luxurious car heading for her junker. She would be embarrassed when he saw it.

Chad nosed the car onto Natividad Road and made his way through traffic to Highway 68, she assumed, back to the field where she'd left her car. They rode in silence, and she realized he hadn't found her a place to stay or he would have told her by now. No matter, she'd get by. God promised to be her strength and shield. He wouldn't let her down.

"Thank you for looking for housing for me. I know it's not easy. I've made it so far, and I'll be just fine. You've been so kind."

He glanced her way, his hands resting on the wheel without the death grip she'd seen on the way to the hospital. "I'm sorry I couldn't come up with one of the government units or the motels—"

"I know. I tried to find one myself. They're hard to come by, too." She heard sadness in his voice.

"But I've found another solution. I hope you'll be okay with it. It's not exactly what you'd planned."

She'd had no plan, but she was pleased he gave her credit for having one. Living day by day, surviving, was her way of life. As the thought filled her, his words traveled through her mind. "What do you mean another solution?"

"I've found a job for you. A housekeeping job where you can have the baby with you." He glanced at her again as if wanting to see her expression. "Is that okay?"

Okay? It was wonderful. A real house, and housekeeping— she could do that with ease. "That sounds very nice, but where will I—"

"You'll have your own room there."

He'd answered her question before she asked it. She sat stunned. Her own room. A room for Nate and her to live in, in a real house. Yet how had he arranged this? She opened her mouth to ask, then stopped herself. She assumed this was temporary, until she could find something more appropriate for her and Nate, but while she could she would be thrilled to live in a real house.

Felisa recognized the area and knew they were near the field she'd been working when she went into labor. Chad pulled down the road, and she pointed to her junker, its dull, rusted body causing her to cringe.

"This one?" he asked, pulling alongside it.

She nodded, afraid to speak for fear he'd hear the shame in her voice.

"Where are your things?" he asked, stopping in front of her car.

"In the trunk." She dug into her pocket and took out her keys.

He reached across the driver's seat, and she dropped the keys into his hand.

"We'll pick up your car later," he said, closing the door and vanishing behind her view.

In moments she heard the trunk lifting, the rustle of her belongings, and the lid closing. She eyed Nate, who stirred at the sound but never whimpered.

The driver's door opened, and Chad slipped back inside. "Now we're on our way."

He still hadn't given her any details, and she didn't feel right asking. He would tell her about the family in time. She could only pray they were kind people who would be patient with her. She'd been away from housecleaning and cooking for some time, but she would learn their wishes fast.

Tired, Felisa leaned her head against the seat cushion. The scent of leather wrapped around her, and she ran her hand over the smooth upholstery. She closed her eyes, then heard a click, and soft music drifted from the radio. The lull of the music and hum of the engine drew her into a haze. When she opened her eyes again, she was startled to see they were out of Salinas proper and passing the sign for Toro Park. She straightened.

"Did you have a nice nap?"

Chad's quiet voice startled her. "Was I sleeping?" She looked at the dashboard clock and realized she had slept for a number of minutes. "Where are we going?"

"Corral de Tierra."

Her stomach knotted. Rich people lived there. She hadn't thought. She glanced down at her apparel, still dusty from her day's work in the fields. "I should have changed my clothes."

"Don't worry. No one will care. You can take a bath and freshen up when you get there."

She glanced at the street sign as he made a left turn onto Corral de Tierra Road. His confidence confused her. How did he know what the owners expected or allowed? The questions welled inside her. "How do you know these people?"

He hesitated before answering. "Because it's my home, Felisa. My housekeeper needs a break, and I thought you could give her a hand once you're stronger."

She froze. Had she been wrong? Could this be a ploy to get her son after all? Or to entrap her? She'd heard about men doing horrible things.

"I am strong now. I can work the fields. You don't need to give me a—"

"Felisa." His calm voice mingled with the music. "I'm not kidnapping you. I can hear in your voice you're worried. I want nothing from you. I told you that already. My housekeeper is working too hard, and I decided this was God's way to motivate me to action. I've been putting it off. It's a big house with two little girls that make a mess."

Her heart thundered, wanting him to be telling the truth, yet so afraid. She looked around at the expanse of trees and foothills where large sprawling homes nestled amid the rugged landscape. A golf course appeared on her left, its short clipped grass and rolling hills dotted with flags on poles hanging in the hot sun.

"That's the country club," he said, as if reading her thoughts again.

A prayer rose in her mind, a prayer for protection and peace as he veered left. He slowed, and Felisa gazed at the large Spanish-style home with wrought iron work, terra-cotta roof and stucco exterior, the color of a soft coral sunset. The warm hues looked inviting and safe.

"This is home," he said, pulling into the driveway. He pushed a button, and the garage doors rose. Inside was the pickup that had carried her to the hospital and another sedan. He pulled inside and turned off the ignition. After he opened the trunk, he hurried around to Felisa's door and opened it. "You get Nate while I unload the trunk."

She stood for a moment, scanning the huge garage. It was bigger than the inside of any house she'd been in, and she could only imagine the size of the Garrison home. She opened the rear door, but instead of unlatching the carrier, she unbuckled Nate from the car seat and snuggled him against her chest. Feeling his warm body nestle against hers aroused more emotion than she'd ever allowed herself to feel. His mouth made sucking noises as if he were ready to eat, but she needed the privacy of the house.

"You'll eat soon," she said, pressing her cheek against the baby's.

He gave a tiny mewl.

"We'll go this way," Chad said, motioning her toward a door to the rear of the garage.

She followed, and when he opened it, they stepped into an amazing courtyard with an ornate fountain like one in the plaza of a Mexican village. Her gaze traveled along the covered portico and the many doors leading inside. She'd never seen so many doors and windows, had never seen such a huge mansion.

Chad had lifted some of her boxes from the trunk and followed the tile path to one of the doors. He turned the knob, and the door opened. "I'll give you a key to the room," he said, as he stepped back and motioned her to go inside.

She moved forward and then faltered, seeing the huge room. A large bed stood at the center of the wall across from the doorway. She scanned the room, noticing an easy chair and table, a dresser, a nightstand with a lamp beside the bed and nearby, a cradle. Tears filled her eyes, and she lowered her head, afraid he would see her crying. She prided herself on being strong and didn't want him to think she was weak.

He crossed the room and rested his hand on the cradle. "I hope you don't mind. It's like new." He rubbed his hand along the wooden footboard. "It belonged to one of the children. I didn't know why I kept it, but I do now." He patted the wood and stepped away, as if the cradle had stirred his memories.

"It's beautiful," she said, inching farther into the room toward the crib—pure white with a clean mattress and a colorful blanket folded at the foot. She'd never seen anything so wonderful.

"We'll have to pick up some linens for it and other baby supplies, but this should do for now."

She swallowed her emotion. "It's too kind of you. I have some blankets and baby clothes in the box." She motioned to the carton he still held in his hand.

He looked surprised that he still held the box, and he hurried to set it on the bed.

Nate gave a soft whimper. "He needs to be fed," she said.

He backed away, nearly tripping over a scatter rug. "I should let you alone. You want to get cleaned up and feed Nate." He swung his arm toward a closed door, then headed toward it. "The bathroom is here."

He swung open the door, and from where she stood Felisa could see a bathtub and sink and no other doors—a private bathroom all her own.

"It's small, but you'll find clean towels and clothes."

Small? She couldn't believe he thought it was little. It looked luxurious to her. "It's just fine." His intense look caused her to flush. "It's more than I had ever imagined."

"This is normally a guest room," he said. "The other door is a closet, and the one there is to a hallway that leads into the other rooms of the house." He turned toward the door, then paused as if having an afterthought. "I'll put the rest of your things outside the door so I don't disturb you."

"Thank you, Mr. Garrison. I don't know what to say."

He shook his head with an endearing grin. "Don't say anything, Felisa." He opened the door to the portico and left her standing in the middle of the room, cuddling Nate to her chest.

❧

Chad stepped outside and sucked in a lengthy breath. That had been more difficult than he'd thought. He'd asked Juanita to bring in the crib. It had been purchased for his new baby but never used. Sorrow rippled through him. He'd been unable to give it away, and now he realized the reason why. It had found a worthwhile purpose. Felisa's glowing smile filled his thoughts. The Bible said to show compassion and to help others, but he realized today he was receiving more than he'd given. The smile and joy on her face paid far more than the cost of the crib or the salary he would pay her for her work.

Chad strode back to his car and pulled out the rest of Felisa's belongings from his trunk, then closed the trunk lid and carried the bag and another carton to her doorway. He left them there and headed inside. As he opened the door he could hear the twins' nanny bellowing at the girls, and he cringed at the sound. Instead of quieting, they only followed her example and screamed louder.

He halted in the doorway of the family room in time to see Faith toss a wooden puzzle at her sister. The pieces scattered across the room and blended with the debris strewn across the carpet. "Girls," he said, using the calmest voice he could.

"Daddy!" Joy screeched, racing into his arms. "Faith hit me with the puzzle."

"She missed," he said, "but it's wrong to throw things."

"I've told them that," Mrs. Drake said. "You'd think they didn't have brains in their heads."

Chad tried not to glare at the woman. She'd been the third replacement in the past two years, and he wanted to give her a chance to succeed. He always avoided addressing issues in front of the girls, but he'd remind her later that they were bright enough to know how to rile her.

"Faith," Chad said, holding his arm open to his daughter, "come here."

"No." She was curled into a ball on the wide sofa.

"Faith, please come here."

"I didn't do it."

"I saw you throw the puzzle, but that's not what I asked you. I asked you to come here." He didn't move but waited.

Finally Faith rolled off the sofa and plopped to the floor. She looked at him with that stubborn look both girls seemed to have as if challenging him. He'd learned not to give in.

"Okay, then I'll just tell Joy the news." He pushed back Joy's hair and spoke softly into her ear. He could see Mrs. Drake staring at him with narrowed eyes and Faith getting more curious by the second.

"Really?" Joy exclaimed, her eyes as wide and blue as her mother's had been.

Chad watched Faith rise from the floor and amble across to his side.

"What news?" she asked.

"First, I need an apology to your sister."

"She hit me first," Faith said.

Joy clung to his neck. "I did not, Daddy."

Chad drew both girls into his arms. "Jesus tells us to ask forgiveness for our sins even if we don't know we did them. So I think you both need to say you're sorry to each other, and then for whatever you might have done today, even if it was an accident, you can both be forgiven."

Both girls shook their heads.

Chad shrugged and let them slide from his arms. "Okay, it's your choice. You can have dinner in your room tonight and miss out on everything."

"Daddy, that's not fair." Both voices blended in one litany.

"No one said it was, but you can make a choice. Dinner in your rooms or say I'm sorry and mean it."

They did a staring standoff until Faith relented. "I'm sorry for throwing the puzzle."

Chad waited a moment to see what Joy would do.

"I'm sorry, too," she said.

Chad pulled them back into his arms. "Now that wasn't so hard, was it?"

"What's the news, Daddy?" Faith asked.

"We have a new housekeeper, and she—"

"Where's Juanita going?" Joy asked.

"Nowhere," he said, "but she needs a vacation, and once the new woman is trained, Juanita can have some time for herself."

Nanny made a disapproving sound, and Chad turned his

attention toward her. "Did you want to say something, Mrs. Drake?"

"No, I'm just surprised."

"Perhaps she can give you some help when you're feeling overwhelmed?"

"Overwhelmed? I—I don't need any—I'm just fine with the girls. Thank you."

"Daddy." He felt Joy tugging at his sleeve. "You didn't tell Faith the best part."

"What best part?" Faith whined. "You didn't tell me the best part."

"The housekeeper has a brand-new baby," Chad said.

Mrs. Drake snorted. "Well, I'll be."

Chad turned his attention in her direction. "Mrs. Drake?"

"A newborn?" She drew up her shoulders. "Whose job will that be? I can't imagine—"

"Don't worry about it. Felisa will care for her own child."

"Felisa," she muttered. "You mean she's another—"

"She's a new employee here for the time being. I'll appreciate your giving her a hand learning the ropes." He saw her disapproval in her eyes, but she didn't comment further.

"Can I hold the baby?" Faith asked.

Joy patted his shoulder. "Me, too. I want to hold the baby."

"That will be up to Felisa, but I suspect she'll want the baby to get a little older before she allows anyone to hold him."

"Him?" Joy sounded disappointed.

"Is it a boy?" Faith asked.

Chad gazed at his two look-alike daughters. "A good-looking boy named Nate." Emotion welled in his chest as he pictured the infant. His own son had never had a chance to be held and loved. His own son never had a chance.

four

Felisa slipped into a pair of pants and buttoned her blue and white flowered cotton blouse. Nate had fallen asleep in the cradle after he'd been fed, and she'd enjoyed a relaxing bath, a rarity for her instead of a quick shower. She'd found a bottle of sweet-smelling bubble bath and leaned her back against the tub, enjoying the fragrance and the soothing sway of the water over her tired body. Afterward she'd washed her hair and dried it with fluffy large towels that wrapped around her whole body.

She gazed at Nate for a moment as she closed the last buttons on her blouse, then smoothed a pink shade of lipstick over her lips and looked in the mirror. She felt like Cinderella, visited by a fairy godmother. Today had been more than she could ever have dreamed. Still, she monitored her joy, wondering if she'd find some catch—a snag or problem that would make her realize it had been a nightmare and not a dream. So much of her life had been.

Not wanting to stray too far from Nate, she opened the door and stepped out for a moment into the sunlight. The fountain tinkled into the pool, and she moved closer to sit on the rim and allow the sun to dry her hair. With the door open, she knew she could hear Nate if he cried.

A sound came from behind her, and when she glanced over her shoulder she saw Chad, and behind him two identical little girls. Their light brown hair hung in ponytails and bounced as they skipped her way. She remembered his saying the girls were a handful, but at the moment she could see only their sweet innocence.

"*Hola*," she said, before realizing she'd spoken Spanish.

"Hola," they echoed back to her.

She gave Chad a questioning look.

"Our other housekeeper is Hispanic, too," he said, standing above her.

She rose, then knelt to the girls' level. "What are your names?"

"Joy."

"Faith." The two names almost came out as one.

"From the Bible," Felisa said. "They're very pretty names." She studied the two girls, looking for a clue to their differences but noticed none.

"Faith has a small freckle in the middle of her forehead," Chad said, as if understanding her searching look at his daughters.

Faith pushed away her bangs and grinned.

The grin reminded Felisa of her employer's words—the girls were a handful—and she could see that glint in Faith's eyes.

"Can we see the new baby?" Faith asked, her excitement evident.

Joy jumped beside her and tugged at her blouse. "Please. Can we see him?"

"Girls, don't bug Felisa."

"Please," they sang, dragging the word into a whine.

Felisa rose. "Just for a minute, but you have to be very quiet. He's sleeping."

"We will," they said in chorus.

Both girls tiptoed beside her across the tiles to her door. She opened it farther, and they scooted inside with their father behind them.

The twins ran to the cradle and leaned over the edge. Faith reached in and touched Nate's fingers. Joy followed, patting his cheek.

"He's so tiny," Faith said. The baby grimaced with the sound.

"Girls," Chad whispered, "you said you'd be quiet."

"We are," Faith said, her volume bombarding the room.

Felisa noticed Joy jiggling the crib, and when she looked, Nate had begun to squirm. Felisa covered Joy's hand with hers and pulled it away without saying anything. The girl looked at her with a sweet smile, but Felisa noticed her foot was pushing against the crib legs. "Enough," Felisa said, shooing them toward the door.

Chad shook his head and mumbled he was sorry, but she understood and realized he did have his hands very full. Those girls missed a parent's attention. Chad worked, and their mother was in heaven. They were left all day with hired help—necessary but unfortunate.

"Would you like to see the rest of the house?" Chad asked.

"I would," she said, "but I'm afraid to leave Nate alone."

"We have an intercom system in the house." He stepped inside and showed her the button. "When it's on, any sound in any room will come into the other rooms. We had it installed when the girls were little, and it makes life easier for Juanita and Mrs. Drake, the nanny."

Amazed, Felisa eyed the button. She'd never experienced such a thing.

"You can feel easier now, and we won't be gone long."

She nodded, wondering how the monitor worked. She was nervous about meeting the other servants.

She followed him as the girls raced ahead, their exuberance almost overwhelming. When she stepped inside the vast interior of a ceramic tile foyer, she looked ahead to see a charming breakfast nook set in a bay window looking out to the fountain, and once she'd traveled the nook's length the spacious island kitchen came into view.

"Juanita," Chad said as they entered.

A middle-aged Hispanic woman turned toward him, and when she saw Felisa, her kindly face made her feel welcome. "This must be Felisa." She gave her a friendly nod. "Welcome to the Garrison home."

"Thank you," Felisa said, embarrassed by her gaping as she viewed the modern kitchen. "This is so beautiful."

Juanita looked around as if seeing it in a new light. "It's roomy and a nice place to prepare the family's meals."

Felisa looked at her and then at her employer, her mind swirling with questions. "I don't know my duties. Am I to help with the cooking or only the cleaning?" She settled her gaze on Chad, almost frightened by the modern conveniences that filled the kitchen.

Chad's face flinched with his own confusion. "You'll fill in where needed. I'll let Juanita give you the duties. I want her to have a vacation, and then you'll take care of everything."

She turned her attention to Juanita. Though she'd been pleasant, she wondered if the woman resented her coming here.

"I'll be happy to do that," Juanita said, then turned and gave Felisa a welcoming smile. "I'll show you around after dinner before I leave."

"Leave?" Felisa cringed when she heard her question blurt out into the room, fearing the woman planned to leave on vacation already.

"I live at home," the housekeeper said. "I come early in the morning and go home after dinner."

"I—I didn't know." The response had left Felisa unsettled. She wasn't comfortable being the only employee staying in the home.

"Mrs. Drake, the nanny, lives in the house," Chad said, as if knowing her thoughts. "You'll meet her at dinner. We all eat together, except Juanita, of course."

"Once dinner is on the table, I head home to my family," she said.

The weight lifted from Felisa's shoulders. "You're all so kind. I—"

A small cry stopped her in mid-sentence.

Juanita chuckled. "That's your baby." She pointed to a box attached to the wall. "It's the monitoring system. You must have turned it on."

"I did." Chad said, motioning toward the doorway. "You can go tend to Nate. We'll call you for dinner."

Her heart rose to her throat. She'd be called to dinner. She was invited to sit at his table. The image twirled in her mind. Life had never treated her so kindly.

❧

Chad watched her hurry away, her slender frame vanishing around the corner, her dark hair falling in kinky waves below her shoulders. He felt his pulse react to the attractive woman, and it startled him. He needed to be careful. Juanita was a motherly figure, and the nanny was an ornery woman he'd thought had good skills with children, but Felisa was lithesome and lovely. Much time had passed since a woman had entered his thoughts. Now one had, and she didn't fit into his world. Yet his emotions didn't seem to care.

He pulled his gaze from the doorway and turned his attention to Juanita. "What do you think?"

She gave him a strange look. "She's had a hard life, I'm sure. She appreciates your help."

"Will this work?"

Juanita shrugged. "We'll see. I'll go easy on her until she adjusts with the new baby, but I hope she'll catch on easily. She seems bright enough. She speaks English well."

"I noticed," he said.

"*Mamá*'s here." The sound came over the intercom. "Come here, *mi niño dulce*."

Chad's chest tightened when he heard Felisa call Nate her sweet boy, though he felt uncomfortable hearing her private thought to her child. He looked at Juanita. "I suppose we'd better tell her to turn off the intercom." He walked to the wall and pressed the button, reminding Felisa to turn off the monitor.

In a moment he heard a click and silence. "I'd better get over to the field. I'll leave her in your care." He jammed his hands into his pockets, aware he didn't want to leave, but knowing he must. "We'll have to pick up her car later, and I'm sure she'll need some things for the baby. Maybe I should—"

His heart rose to his throat as he heard his enthusiasm. Chad hadn't felt motivation like this since before his wife died, and it unsettled him. He stole a glance at Juanita, who'd been eyeing him off and on as she worked at the island making a pie.

"I'll say good-bye to the girls and then be going."

He heard Juanita's good-bye as he made his way into the family room, and though the floor looked as if an earthquake had knocked the contents every which way, the girls weren't there. He retraced his steps, then took the hallway into the bedroom wing. A piercing scream gave him direction, and when he came through the doorway he saw the nanny with her fingers clutched around Joy's arm while the other hand pointed in her face.

"What's the problem?" he said, not happy at what he saw.

"These girls must learn to listen. I've asked them to hang up their clothes, and look." She gestured toward the floor and a chair, which had been strewn with garments.

"That's not too much to ask. Joy, if you want dessert tonight, you'll have this mess cleaned up in five minutes. Juanita's making a pie, and it's probably one of your favorites."

"I think Joy should go without dinner," Mrs. Drake said, having pulled her pointing finger from Joy's face but still grasping her arm.

"We'll talk about this later." He took a step backward, then stopped and leveled his gaze at the nanny. "If you let go of her arm, Joy can begin putting away her clothing."

She released her grasp without a word and crossed her arms over her chest as she watched. Chad stood for a moment, seeing his little four-year-old gathering the garments and dropping them on the bed. He'd made closets with hangers low enough for the girls to reach. He knew they needed to learn tasks, but seeing the look in their nanny's eyes didn't set well with him. They did need to talk.

He passed Faith's room and saw her sitting in the middle of the floor working a puzzle. She loved puzzles, and, seeing her so quiet for once, he didn't want to disturb her so he tiptoed past and made his way to the garage, his mind tumbling with thoughts.

Pulling the car keys from his pocket, Chad stood for a moment, aware of the strange sensations reeling through him. Felisa had stirred memories he'd tried to keep in check. She'd stirred the love he'd felt for his wife and for his stillborn child as he watched her with her own son. The tiny bundle of life aroused his paternal feelings, and he didn't know how to handle them.

He dismissed his thoughts, climbed into the truck, and backed out of the garage into the street. As he drove, Felisa's image rose in his mind. He'd watched her gentleness with his girls. She hadn't shown anger when the twins misbehaved by the crib. She'd taken control and guided them away with patience.

His twins. The two matching faces replaced Felisa's image.

Maybe he hadn't been a good father. He'd grieved so long for his wife and son that perhaps the girls had sensed it. Had they felt rejected when he sank into his sullen moods? They'd gone through one nanny after another. None had been able to find a way to reach the girls, and he couldn't stay home and do it himself. He had a business—a huge farm to run, his livelihood. It gave them a good life, a very good life, he admitted.

Yet he had to beware. He wanted to turn around and drive back home. He wanted to take Felisa shopping for baby clothes and baby bottles, shopping for all the wonderful things he could afford to lavish on the little boy, but she'd halted him with her comment; she had a carton of used items. How could he insist the child have new things when she had learned to live with hand-me-downs and accepted them with no regrets?

His way of life was so different. Yet he longed to share that life. . .with someone.

❧

Felisa lit the candles in her room and knelt at the side of her bed for her morning prayers. She looked at the picture of Jesus she'd hung on the wall and smiled. He had provided for her as He always had. Knowing she had someone to count on, someone who stood by her side, made all the difference.

After a week in the Garrison home, she'd begun to relax. She'd learned her way around the house, helped Juanita in the kitchen, and felt blessed at the wonderful life God was allowing her to lead. Juanita had been gracious, and only the nanny made her feel out of place. She thanked the Lord for all the gifts she'd received—the good food, the comfortable bed, the friend she'd found in Juanita—and she asked Him to be with her each day.

As the amen faded, Felisa's mind drifted to Chad. She

needed to thank the Lord for the gift of an employer who cared. She knew Chad was a Christian, not only by the prayers they said at dinner, but by the faith he showed in his actions. She knew she was saved by grace through faith, but she also knew the Bible said faith without deeds was dead. Chad Garrison was a man of faith. She had no doubt.

Felisa rose from her knees, blew out the candles, then opened the blinds on her windows. The sun spilled through the window, throwing lines of shade and light on the carpeting. She walked to the crib and looked down at her son, who seemed to be smiling up to her.

"*Te amo*, Nate, my little *muchacho*," she said, expressing her love as she reached down and lifted him against her chest. He'd already eaten, and he looked content. "Want to see the sunlight?" She carried him to the door and pulled it open, letting the warmth float through the screen. She stood there for a moment listening to the splatter of the fountain and nothing more. The hush of this quiet place amazed her. They were far from other neighbors, many blocked from view by the rolling foothills and masses of trees that covered the mountainsides.

Once she'd settled Nate into his carrier chair, she headed for the house. Juanita had been very cooperative and allowed her to work with the baby alongside her. She grabbed a piece of toast from the kitchen and began her tasks for the day, cleaning the master bedroom and bath. She left Nate with Juanita while she gathered her supplies to take to the rooms; then she would return.

The master bedroom amazed her the few times she'd seen it. Felisa set her basket of cleaning equipment on the floor near the door and gazed at the spacious room. The deep brown carpeting spread across the expansive floor, and a wide window looked out to the rich mountain scenery. She gazed at the stone fireplace, a large built-in television, and a bed that could hold five people. She shook her head at the wasted space, but she loved the thought of having all this room for oneself.

Behind the fireplace wall was the bathroom with a large sunken tub. She could only imagine such luxury. A shower stood nearby, and a gigantic closet he could walk into. It could hold so many clothes that it, too, seemed wasted space.

She hurried back to retrieve Nate from Juanita's caring hands, then delved into her work. Pride filled her as she dusted and polished the room, scrubbed the bathroom porcelain, vacuumed the floors, and shined the mirrors. She paused at the wide mirror to study her face. She witnessed the same glow of happiness on her countenance that also burned in her heart.

The thought expanded and then popped like a pin-poked balloon. Once accustomed to this good life, how could she ever go back to the cheap motels and nights in her car? This was a dream world where she didn't belong, and the longer she stayed the worse it would be to go back.

Felisa sank to the tub's edge and put her face into her hands. As much as she longed to stay, she must leave. Nate seemed healthy and happy. He had been a good baby from birth, and she could carry him on her back in a sling and still work the fields. She had to tell her employer. She had to tell him soon.

Tears welled in her eyes. She'd allowed her imagination to grow, and sometimes she even pictured herself as the wife of the manor. Foolish dreams could only hurt her, and she knew his world would reject her as fast as Mrs. Drake had.

Pushing away her meandering thoughts, Felisa worked at her tasks while keeping an eye on Nate. She finished the master bedroom and bath. Then after lunch, she moved into the breakfast nook and the foyer. Keeping the tile shining seemed an eternal job, and the twins popped up everywhere, always underfoot.

Felisa wondered why the nanny didn't have a better understanding of the little girls. She never saw her play with them or read to them. Instead the woman snarled instructions and jerked them to get their attention. She didn't want to see that, and she wondered why the nanny remained employed. When she asked, Juanita said Mrs. Drake was the third nanny in the past two years. Something seemed wrong. Two little girls needed love and attention, not punishment.

Punishment. If anyone should punish, it would be God. Everyone deserved punishment, but instead the Lord granted forgiveness and eternal life. Everyone needed love and security. They needed hope. These two little girls needed the same. If God could forgive His children's sins, then Mrs. Drake should be able to overlook two little precocious girls' antics.

Today Juanita didn't need help with dinner, so Felisa took advantage of the lovely day and pulled a chair from the umbrella table to sit beside the fountain. As she settled with Nate at her side in his carrier and began to sing him a Mexican lullaby, footsteps sounded on the tiles beneath the portico, and the twins came darting toward her.

"Let's play!" Joy shouted.

"We have puzzles," Faith added, dropping pieces as she skittered toward Felisa. The child stopped and scooped up the puzzle pieces, then continued to scurry toward her.

"You should sit at the table," Felisa said, gesturing toward the round table just outside the shade of the covered porch.

"We want to do it here with you and Nate," Joy said, plopping at her feet.

Felisa drew in a lengthy breath, then grinned, knowing her short relaxation had ended. Before she could steer them to the table, Faith had joined Joy on the tiles at her feet, and they'd begun to argue.

"Do you like people hollering at you?" Felisa asked.

Their entangled voices silenced, and two faces tilted up to her.

"No," they both said in unison.

"Then why are you yelling at each other?"

Faith put her hands on her hips. "But we're—"

"You're yelling."

Faith wrinkled her nose. "We don't like Nanny yelling at us."

"I don't like you hollering at me," Joy said, glaring at her sister.

"Do you know why we don't like it?" Felisa asked.

Both girls raised their eyes to her.

"Because everyone likes to be respected, and we can't be respectful when we yell. How do you think we can be respectful?"

Both heads lowered for a moment until Joy raised hers. "We listen?"

"Right," Felisa said, giving her a smile. "We listen to what the other person has to say."

"I listen," Faith said.

Felisa tousled her hair and decided to take the lesson one step further. "But only when you want to. We have to be willing to listen to each other and then ask ourselves if the person has been honest. Jesus wants us to cooperate with one another and to be honest." She picked up one of the puzzles and held it out to them. "Who brought this puzzle outside?"

"I did," Joy said, grasping the puzzle piece and leaping up.

Faith clasped two of them against her chest. "These are mine."

"I see three puzzles. Instead of arguing, you could each work on your own and then trade when you're done, or. . ."

She paused to let them think.

Faith flashed her a grin. "Or we could do one at a time and each take turns putting in a piece."

Felisa clapped her hands. "Right. That's a great answer. So which do you want to do?"

"We want you to work the puzzle with us," Joy said, leaning against her as if she were a lamppost.

Felisa slipped her arm around the girl's waist.

Faith tugged at her pant leg. "We'll take turns." She patted her hand against the tiles as if inviting her to join them on the ground.

Looking heavenward, Felisa sent up a little prayer of thanks. Before she could join them a noise caught her attention, and she spotted Mrs. Drake standing in the shadow of the portico, arms akimbo, staring at her with narrowed eyes. The woman didn't like her at all, and she could do nothing to change that. She'd tried.

She turned away and shifted to the tiles beside the girls. They liked her. Juanita liked her, too, and her employer seemed to care. What more did she need?

five

Chad stepped from the garage into the sunlight. When his eyes adjusted, he paused, looking at the startling sight. Felisa sat on the tiles near the fountain between his daughters, playing a game, and they were so intent, they hadn't seen or heard him arrive. He moved closer and realized they were working jigsaw puzzles. His heart soared at the sight. Normally he arrived home to the girls' voices bellowing their complaints and arguments, but today his ears picked up only their happy voices and playful giggles.

He stood in the distance, watching Felisa with the girls. He heard her soft laughter and tender voice as she spoke to them. He heard Joy beg her to sing them a song, and Felisa shook her head no, but soon her clear voice lifted in an old Mexican folk song he recalled hearing among the field workers. He didn't move, not wanting to break the spell.

When she finished, the girls spoke in soft voices, and he ambled nearer.

"Daddy!" Joy sang out, jumping from her play and dashing toward him. Faith soon followed, and he wrapped his arms around the girls while his gaze lingered on Felisa, who sat where she'd been, smiling up at him.

He clutched the girls' hands in his and guided them back to Felisa, then stood above the carrier, admiring the beautiful boy. "Do you mind?" he asked, gesturing to Nate.

"Not at all," she said.

He crouched and lifted the child into his arms, smiling at the infant's tiny fists flailing in the air. A warm sense of love flooded him. He rose and gazed at his daughters, quiet and happy by Felisa's side, and then again at the baby boy against his chest. The child flung his arm upward, then lowered it and jammed his fist into his mouth.

"He's hungry," Felisa said, seeing Nate suckling at his fingers. "I should take him inside."

She moved beside Chad, and the sweetness of her scent enfolded him. He drew in the aroma, letting it rush through his senses. He gave her a nod, though hating to let the child go. He brushed his lips against the baby's cheek, then nestled him back into the carrier. He glanced at his watch. "It's nearly dinnertime. Can I carry him inside for you?"

"You don't have to," she said, her voice as stirring as a mountain breeze.

"I don't mind," he said, hoisting the carrier into his arms and carrying it toward her door.

The girls rose and scampered along with them and dashed inside as soon as Felisa held open the door.

"Outside, girls," Chad said, setting the carrier beside the crib. "We have to get ready for dinner, and Felisa needs to feed the baby."

"Can we help?" Joy asked, leaning over the carrier and tickling Nate beneath the chin.

"Not this time, Joy," Felisa said, giving the girls a pat. "Soon he'll be older, and then you can—then you could help."

Chad watched her expression change to sadness. What had happened to cause her unhappiness? He lingered for a moment, wanting to ask, but the baby's whimper and the twins' exuberance gave him a nudge. "We'll see you at dinner."

"Thank you," she said, her voice as wistful as her look.

Chad beckoned the girls through the doorway, his emotions tangling with concern.

The girls raced on ahead and nearly ran over Mrs. Drake,

who stood in the shadow of the portico watching him.

He studied her as he approached, seeing darkness in her eyes, and he figured he was ready to hear her "bad girls" report he received so often. "Did you want to see me?" he asked.

"I certainly do," she said, her gaze drifting from him toward Felisa's room. "I'm not comfortable with that woman being here. She's trying to undermine my relationship with the twins, and it's making things more difficult for me, Mr. Garrison."

He studied her dire expression, trying to understand her complaint. "What has she done?"

"I try to discipline them, and the next thing I find is her sitting outside with them playing games. Naturally they would rather stay there than do the tasks I ask them to do."

"I'm sorry. I don't understand. I would think you'd be pleased when the girls are amused and not under your feet."

She folded her arms over her chest. "Children need to follow rules. They need discipline, not a playmate."

Chad shook his head. "Joy and Faith are four years old. Do you realize this is the time of life children enjoy playing? I expect them to mind and to do reasonable tasks. They need to learn to hang up their clothes. I support you on that, but I see no harm in their playing outside, and if Felisa is playing with them, I don't mind at all."

"I thought she was the housekeeper. Isn't she supposed to be doing her job?"

"I assume she had finished her work, but I'll check with Juanita."

"Juanita? They're two of a kind. You won't get an honest—"

This time he glared at her. "I have every confidence in Juanita. She's been employed by my family for many years. I'll check with her, and thank you for your concern."

He held his ground while Mrs. Drake stomped away,

muttering under her breath.

Chad didn't move. He stood in the silence, pondering what had just occurred. Was it jealousy or true concern? He didn't want the girls to be rude to the nanny; yet he knew they responded better to affection, and they received little from Mrs. Drake.

Guilt slid down his back as he thought of the many hours he spent away from the children when they really needed him. He wished he could put his trust in Joe to keep things moving smoothly while he took a short vacation. Joe had been a hard worker and had done nothing to lose his trust, so why not? Maybe he would take a week off to spend time with the girls. He could even take a day or two and focus on the twins. They could go to the beach in Carmel, and he could stop by his store. He hadn't been there recently, and the trip could serve two purposes.

He pulled back his shoulders, excited about the venture. He wondered if Felisa had ever enjoyed a day in Carmel on the long stretch of white sand. Perhaps she would join them. The thought prickled down his arms. It wasn't appropriate to take her, he supposed—the employer and his housekeeper going out for the day. He tilted his head and looked from beneath the portico to the blue sky. *Lord, help me. My heart is leading me in one direction, and wisdom is leading me in the other. You're both heart and mind—love and wisdom. Help me make sense out of my feelings and lead me in the way I should go.* He whispered an amen into the sunshine, then headed inside to talk with Juanita.

❧

Felisa gazed at Nate waking from his nap, his tiny arms waving above his head at a mobile the twins had given him—one that had been theirs when they were babies. Nate loved the twirling figures that danced above his head when he awakened in the morning or from his naps. Her stomach growled, letting her know she'd better get in to eat dinner now that Nate had awakened. Juanita would be cleaning up and getting ready to go home.

The room felt cool, and Felisa was amazed at how the heat of the day seemed blocked by the stucco walls. She walked to the door and pulled it open to let in the light. Instead she saw two matching faces standing outside looking at the door. Both girls bounced and clapped when they saw her.

"So why this happy greeting?" Felisa asked, curious as to their excitement.

Joy shielded her eyes and pressed her nose against the screen. "Daddy said we could make a piñata tonight."

"Where's Nate?" Faith asked, following Joy's determination to look inside her room.

"He's watching the lovely gift you gave him." She gestured toward the colorful mobile, then addressed Joy's comment. "Do you know how to make a piñata?"

Joy giggled. "No, but you do."

"I thought so," she said, gazing at the two eager faces. "I'll talk to your daddy. We'll make a mess, you know."

"He said we could make it on the porch." Faith pointed to the covered portico.

"I'll still check with him first before I say yes or no."

"Okay," they said in unison, then backed away and scampered toward the house.

Felisa settled Nate into the baby carrier and headed inside. She wanted to talk with Chad, but not about piñatas. With the girls' eagerness, she feared she wouldn't get a moment alone with him.

When she stepped into the back foyer, her heart rose to her throat. Chad was still seated in the breakfast nook, reading the evening paper. She forced herself forward, her emotions torn between running away and running toward him. He gave her the greatest sense of security she'd ever felt, and besides he made her pulse flutter. She hadn't felt that since she'd first laid eyes on Miguel before she knew his faults. Then her pulse only raced from fear of Miguel's temper and nothing more.

"Hungry?" Chad asked, looking up. "How's the little muchacho?"

"He's a good boy," she said, resting him beside a chair before heading into the kitchen and greeting Juanita.

The housekeeper chuckled. "I'm guessing the girls have already talked to you about their plans."

Felisa grinned. "About making a piñata."

"They've been after me about those things since you talked to them." Juanita handed her a dish and motioned to the food on a warming plate. "Have some dinner."

"*Gracias.*" Felisa lifted a cheese quesadilla from the platter and shifted it onto her plate, then spooned fresh fruit beside it.

"Would you like a cup of coffee?" Juanita motioned toward a mug. "I brewed caffeinated. I think you'll need your energy tonight with the girls."

"You mean making piñatas?"

Juanita gave her a grin and nodded.

Felisa headed toward the breakfast nook, but uncomfortable with imposing on Chad's privacy, she passed him and made her way to the outside umbrella table.

"Where are you going?" Chad asked.

"I thought I'd eat outside. I'll be back for Nate in a minute."

"Sit here. By the time you do all that, your food will be cold." He rose and pulled out a chair for her.

His gaze captured hers, and her heart pounded. His eyes flickered with emotion she hadn't expected, a look so tender and warm it washed through her. She sank to the chair, set her plate on the table, then looked down at Nate. "You're such a good baby."

Chad had folded his paper, and it sat beside him. "Do you mind if I hold him?"

"Go ahead," she said, confused by his preoccupation with her son.

He crouched and unhooked the baby, then lifted him to his chest. "He's growing already, and look at him grin." He tilted the baby toward Felisa.

She chuckled. "I think it's gas."

"That's okay. If I can get a smile, I'll take the gas, too." He settled back into the chair and bent down to kiss the baby's cheek.

Chad's tenderness sent emotion stirring in Felisa's chest. She wished she understood why a rugged, hardworking man showed so much delight in an infant. Usually men seemed to steer clear of babies. She recalled so many who would do anything rather than feed or diaper a child.

She lifted the quesadilla with her fingers. The cheese oozed onto the plate, and when she took a bite, amid the sharp cheddar she tasted the smoky crispness of bacon. She licked her lips and noticed Chad watching her. Her stomach twisted, her food forming a lump. She had this moment, and she needed to use it. "I wanted to talk with you about—"

"The piñata," he said. "I know. I'm sorry, but the girls have been bugging me all evening." He grinned. "Every minute, actually, since they learned you know how to make them. I told them it was your decision if you wanted to do it tonight." He gave her the sweetest, guiltiest grin she'd ever seen while he nestled Nate in his arms and gave him tiny pats as he swayed with him.

Before she could respond, the girls bounded into the room.

"Did you ask him?" Faith asked, jiggling beside her chair.

"I did—"

"Daddy," Joy said, clinging to his arm, "you're always holding Nate." She gave him a questioning look.

"I held you and Faith just like this when you were babies."

"You did?" they both said at the same time.

The girls hovered around him, eating up the attention, and it filled Felisa's heart to see the joy in their faces. This was what they needed—wonderful times with their dad so he could show his love and concern for them. She missed that, too, as a girl, but then that was life for many of the children from hardworking families. Too many kids and too little money.

"What about the piñata?" Faith asked again, shifting her focus back to Felisa.

"Isn't it late?"

"The sun's still shining," Faith said. "Daddy?"

He grinned at Faith and then at Felisa. "Felisa can spend the evening as she wishes."

"Do you wish to make a piñata?" Joy pleaded.

Felisa burst into laughter. "You girls certainly know how to nag."

"Isn't that part of a woman's charm?" Chad said, his husky voice sending quivers down her back.

"Okay, we'll make a piñata," she said, avoiding his comment, "but they make a mess."

"We'll clean up," Faith said.

"We promise." Joy hung onto her arm.

Chad's voice broke through the girls' exuberance. "And I'll watch Nate. How's that for a deal?"

"Okay," Felisa said, realizing her goal of a private talk had faded away.

Juanita came out to say good-bye as she left for home, so with Chad tending to Nate, Felisa gathered the supplies—

flour, water, newspapers, and string—and carried them to the umbrella table. She sent the girls to find a large balloon they said was left over from their last birthday party a couple of months earlier.

When they returned, Felisa drew in a deep breath. "Now you know we can only shape part of it today. It has to dry for a few days before we can make anything."

"Okay," they chimed in.

"Here's what we do." She turned to Chad. "You can blow up this balloon for me, and, girls, you can mix the paste." While Chad worked on the balloon, she emptied two cups of flour into a large basin and poured in three cups of water. "Now we need to mix this until it's smooth."

The girls dived into the job, cooperating as she'd never seen them do before. She noticed their father watching, his eyes twinkling with joy at seeing his two mischievous girls working so hard.

Felisa opened the newspaper and tore the sheets into long strips.

"Is this good?" Joy asked.

Felisa dipped her fingers into the pasty substance and gave them a smile. "Good job." She glanced at Chad, who held the balloon pinched between his fingers.

"I can't put a knot in it." He nodded his head toward the baby.

Chuckling, Felisa took the long length of string and knotted it around the balloon; then for good measure she held Nate while Chad knotted the balloon again. With a smile, they traded the balloon for the baby.

"Now it's time to work. What will we make? A star? A burro? A flower?"

"What's a burro?" Joy asked.

"It's a donkey," Chad answered.

Joy curled up her nose. "I want a star."

Faith folded her arms across her chest and yelled, "I want a flower!"

"Hmm?" Felisa said. "We have only one balloon and two votes. Which voice wins? The very loud, mean voice or the soft, happy voice?" She raised an eyebrow at Faith, who squirmed beneath her gaze. "Which voice did we like the best, Daddy?" She turned her gaze to Chad, and her stomach yo-yoed with the look.

"I think the happy voice wins today. We'll make a star."

Faith's lips puckered as if she were going to whine, but she seemed to think for a minute before reacting. "Next time can we do a flower?"

She had used her sweetest voice, and Felisa was filled with relief and happiness. "Yes, we can do that for sure."

ᔨ

Chad's heart swelled as he watched Felisa with his daughters. She knew the right thing to say and seemed to love the girls despite their behavior. He'd noticed them changing since they'd spent time with Felisa. With Mrs. Drake, they attacked each other over every issue, but Felisa knew how to guide them to good decisions. He sent up a prayer, thanking God for her stepping into their lives. She'd brought joy and peace to the house, making it more a home than it had been since Janie had died.

Thinking of Janie, Chad turned his gaze to Nate, wondering how he would have felt holding his own son in his arms, seeing him grow and become a toddler. Years later he would have grown into a young man and one day would have begun to date and would want the family car. A bittersweet grin tugged at his mouth.

He leaned back, surrounded by the scent of baby powder and milk, as he held the tiny infant against his chest. But soon the baby's fragrance was covered by the mixture of flour, water, and wet newspaper the girls had helped prepare.

Felisa amazed him. Her patience with the twins touched his heart, and he made a decision that if Mrs. Drake threatened one more time to leave his employ, he would replace her with Felisa. She seemed to be doing most of the work lately anyway.

He watched the piñata take shape. Layers and layers of pasted paper wrapped around the balloon. The girls' clothing and faces were gooped with the adhesive, but they looked so excited, he couldn't complain.

"That's about it," Felisa said, stepping back and looking at the lumpy newspaper orb. "Now we use this piece of string to hang it outside in the sun where it can dry."

"How long?" Faith asked.

"A couple of days. We'll have to see."

"I can't wait," Joy said, grinning at the misshapen paste ball.

Chad's heart felt light, and an idea flashed in his mind. "Let's say we get you girls ready for bed, and since Mrs. Drake is off tomorrow, we'll all go into Carmel for a trip to the beach."

Felisa glanced his way. "You'll enjoy that." She gave them each a squeeze. "I've never been to the beach at Carmel. I've never really been—"

"Then you'll enjoy it, too," Chad said, watching her expression switch to surprise.

"Me?" She touched her finger to her chest. "But I thought you meant the—"

"You thought wrong. I meant all of us. We'll buy a picnic lunch at my store."

She drew back. "Your store?"

"I have a shop in town that sells sandwiches and grocery items. People love to pick up a lunch and head down to the beach or eat in the park. We'll take chairs to sit on."

"And a blanket," Faith said. "And beach toys."

"We'll take blankets and toys, too." He listened to their exuberance until Nate's cry captured his attention. "What's wrong, Nate?" Chad gave him gentle pats on the back.

"It's his bedtime, and he's hungry, too," Felisa said. "It's past his feeding time."

Chad sent the girls a grin, then rose, gave the crying Nate a tiny squeeze, and handed him to Felisa. "I'll get these two off for bed, and you can take care of this sad fellow."

"Are you sure you want us to go?" She gave him an apologetic look and clutched the crying baby to her chest. "I never know if Nate will be cranky."

Her face filled with question, and her sacrifice touched him. "I've never been surer." He gave her hand a pat, and the touch filled him with longing. The sensation startled him. He knew he cared about Nate and had compassion for Felisa, but today he became aware of his growing feelings. She'd become more to him than a housekeeper and a woman who needed help. Chad realized he needed help, too. He wanted to live again, for himself and for his two sweet girls, who deserved a parent who was truly alive.

six

On Saturday Felisa felt excited as Chad parked the car by the white sand and the sparkling blue-green water. She slipped Nate into the stroller, still astounded that one baby seat could also be a carrier and a stroller. Chad's gift had been wonderful, but too extravagant. The girls skipped along as they headed toward his store. Chad had pointed it out earlier as they drove down to the ocean, and she'd noticed the nearby park, too.

The walk from the beach was uphill, but she enjoyed the exercise. She glanced into the charming shops with gifts and women's fashion filling the display windows. A nature shop had caught the girls' interest, and Felisa wished she had enough money to go inside and buy the twins a gift. As they passed a luggage store, the scent of leather filled her senses, followed by the aroma of candles drifting through another doorway.

In the next block, she eyed jewelry in the displays, and as she moved farther along the sidewalk, she saw wonderful sparkling gems and shiny gold. Then a quaint quilt-maker's shop came into view. She'd never seen so many people meandering along as if they had no place to go and no care in the world. This was a life she would never know.

Chad pointed ahead, and she looked up and saw the sign: GARRISON'S GROCERIES AND DELI. He nodded when she smiled, and the look on his face made her smile back. Inside the shop, Chad was greeted by the manager and introduced her to a couple of workers behind the counter. He introduced her as Felisa Carrillo, with no mention that she was his housekeeper. She saw one worker give her a questioning look, but she turned her attention to the luncheon meats.

When Chad finished talking, they all chose their sandwiches. She and Chad selected pita bread stuffed with ham, salami, and cheese with shredded lettuce and a special sauce, while the girls wanted plain ham and mustard sandwiches on white bread. Chad grabbed a large bag of potato chips, and the girls picked out their favorite cookies. When he pulled out his wallet, the clerk grinned and motioned him on. He laughed and tucked his wallet back into his pocket. He waved, and they followed him outside into the bright sunshine.

Chad halted on the sidewalk. "We could eat at the park, but I thought—"

"At the beach, Daddy," Faith said, bouncing beside him.

"Please," Joy intoned while she clung to the bag of chips.

He glanced at Felisa, and she gave him a willing nod, happy to return to the white sand and the breeze drifting from the wonderful blue-green water. She'd never seen anything so lovely.

The walk back to the beach seemed easier to Felisa, and the closer they came to the ocean the more she felt overjoyed. She drew in deep breaths of salty air and listened to the gulls squawk as they dipped and soared overhead. She eyed the gnarled Monterey pines dotting the beach with their twisted branches. Though they looked dead, she knew they had life. That was how she had felt for so long, dead to the world. Yet God had given her back a life so amazing it made her heart feel as if it would burst.

They stopped at the car for blankets and chairs and to change Nate's diaper. She cuddled him to her side, knowing he'd never remember this day, but she would. Always. When her feet touched the sand, Felisa slipped off her shoes and let her toes sink into the white crystals. Chad gestured to an empty area and opened the chairs while the girls spread out the blankets. They unpacked the sacks holding their lunch, then bowed their heads as Chad prayed. Felisa felt close to God here, just as she felt God's presence in all of nature from every lettuce head to the smoky purple rise of mountains.

"What do you think?" Chad asked, gesturing toward the wide expanse of ocean and beach.

"It's so beautiful. I've never seen anything like this before. I never had the time or the mon—" She stopped herself. This was no time to moan about her lack of finances. No matter how kind, Chad Garrison was her employer, and he might think she was asking for more.

He washed down a bite of sandwich with some soda, then grinned. "I'm glad you're enjoying this. I can't thank you enough for all you've done for us." He tilted his head toward the girls. "You've added something special to our home that's been missing for too long."

She felt herself frown. She couldn't make sense out of that. What could he be missing in that wonderful home?

"You don't understand?" he asked.

She shook her head.

"Laughter, for one."

Laughter? No one had ever thanked her for laughter. What about her housekeeping? "I hope I'm cleaning well enough for you. If I'm missing anything, please let me know. I—"

He reached out and touched her hand. "I have no complaints at all, Felisa. I'm telling you that you're not only working well for us, but you're giving the girls and me so much more than I can ever repay."

The girls and me? She'd given the girls her time, but what had she given him? "Living in your home is gift enough for me. Thank you for trusting in me."

He smiled, but beneath the smile, she sensed he had more to say.

"Can we play now?" Faith asked, wiping her hands on a paper napkin.

"Down by the water?" Joy added.

Chad looked toward the water, then back at the girls. "Okay. Let's go." He sent Felisa a grin and hoisted himself from the chair.

"Goody!" They sprang up and pulled off their bathing-suit covers. They dropped them on the blanket and skittered across the sand to the water's edge with Chad behind them.

Felisa laughed when Faith put one toe in the water and jumped back. Joy did the same when she sank her toe in the water. Felisa couldn't hear what they were saying because of the surf hitting the shore, but she knew they were calling to her that the water was cold.

In minutes they moved back to the damp sand, and the twins began building a castle or a fort—Felisa couldn't tell. But they were busy at their task and working together. She was pleased to see the girls getting along so well lately.

"Look at them," Chad said, returning to his chair. "This has happened since you came." He shifted his gaze to hers. "That's what I mean. You've touched our lives with something special. I look forward to coming from work at night to a home with laughter instead of a house with angry voices."

"I like your girls, Mr. Garrison."

He drew back and eyed her. "Mr. Garrison sounds so strange for some reason. I know it's proper, but when we're alone, would you please call me Chad?"

Her skin prickled with his request. She'd called him Chad in her mind but never aloud. She knew it wasn't right, but she felt so close to him. "I'm not sure that's—"

"Mrs. Drake would be unhappy, I know, but in private she'll

never know. I'm not happy with—" He faltered and shook his head. "You'd make me happy by calling me Chad."

Felisa felt her heart in her throat and could only nod. Nate let out a cry and, grateful for his intrusion, she lifted him into her arms and cuddled him against her.

Chad glanced away, then rose. "I'd better see to the girls."

He strode toward them while Felisa remained with Nate in her arms. She'd been stunned to hear his request and his kind words. He'd almost admitted his frustration with Mrs. Drake. She'd seen it on his face, but it wasn't appropriate for him to admit it. Felisa didn't like the woman, either. She seemed more concerned about the children's training than she did about their happiness. The girls needed a balance of both. Discipline and love worked miracles on them. She'd seen that happen today.

Nate let out another cry, this time without letup, and Felisa knew he would want to eat. She'd made the decision earlier to take him into the car when it was time, and when Chad turned to gaze at her, she signaled him where she was going, and he waved. With her feet slipping in the sand, she hurried to the nearby car and climbed into the backseat. Nate was eager for his feeding, and as he nestled in her arms, Felisa gazed out the window and watched Chad with the twins.

Felisa had wanted to see Chad become an active, loving father, and her prayer had been answered. He'd come to life today. He knelt beside the girls, his strong back bent over their attempts to make a sand castle. She could see his firm jaw relax in a smile, and when his head tilted back in laughter, she felt a smile grow on her face. She released a sigh, longing to let her heart open to the emotions that jarred her with awareness. She had to be grateful for Chad's friendship even though it had to be hidden from the others who worked for him.

Chad stood and looked across the water, and Felisa wondered what he was thinking. Perhaps his thoughts were on his work. She knew he had a good business sense. His farm managers had always treated the help well. His wealth was obvious from the look of his home and by the shop here in Carmel. She'd never had an opportunity before to see how the other side lived. Felisa had come to realize that even with money they, too, had their lives stressed with worries and their hearts broken.

Felisa glanced at her watch, wondering when they would leave. The girls had already bugged her on the way to Carmel about finishing the piñata even if it was wet. If awards were given for nagging, Faith especially would win the gold medal. She chuckled, realizing she, too, was anxious to see the results of their handiwork.

Her opportunity to talk with Chad had died with the girls' interruption, and now Felisa didn't want to talk about leaving. She needed to think and pray about it. Chad had made her feel welcome and needed, a feeling she'd never experienced before now. Her son needed good care, and the housekeeper job gave her that opportunity. She would have to remind herself each day that she didn't fit into the Garrison world. She would have to guard her heart.

❧

Chad watched the ocean rolling in, the tide tugging at the sand beneath his feet. Life seemed the same sometimes, problems and worries making him lose balance, the beauty in front of him marred by the things that lashed against him like waves on a stormy sea. Today the tide only played games with the sand. The water rolled to shore in rounded waves like corrugated paper.

He listened to his daughters' laughter and saw their contentment in playing together, and he glanced toward his car, where Felisa nursed her beautiful son. His heart filled with God's blessings; yet something inside told him to beware. Hearts could be broken. If the twins became too attached to Felisa, they would be hurt when she left. He jammed his hands into his pockets, admitting he would be hurt, as well. Why had his heart turned into mush? Was it because Nate reminded him of his own little boy? Was it the woman whose vulnerable eyes sent shivers down his back? Could it be a little of both?

He turned to see Felisa returning to her chair, her attention focused on the little one in her arms. When she looked up he waved, and she waved back, her smile as bright as the late afternoon sun. He eyed his watch. They needed to head home soon. The sun had begun its slow journey toward its familiar soft coral glow over the horizon, and later, when it vanished beneath the amazing stretch of blue, the breeze would chill.

God gave His children lessons through nature. Even the brightest moment could dim with dark worries and problems. He'd felt in darkness for the past two years. The light had finally broken through his deadened heart. His girls needed him, he knew, and for once he felt ready to admit he needed someone, too.

❧

The following Saturday Felisa rose from her prayers and stretched her arms over her head. She'd had a wonderful time with Chad and the girls a week earlier, and she felt as happy this weekend had arrived, although she'd been disappointed when Chad told her he had to work. Felisa wanted to talk with him. Something inside nudged her to go back to her hard life in the fields. She had prayed every day for God's guidance, and she wasn't sure if was the Lord prodding her or her own fear.

Since she'd arrived, Felisa sensed Mrs. Drake would do

anything, even lie, to get her out of the house, and she also worried about her feelings for Chad. She felt drawn to him. When she watched him with Nate, her heart nearly burst, and though the girls had their moments, she'd grown to love them.

Last Tuesday they'd finished the star piñata, and on Thursday Faith had coerced her into making the other piñata, this one a flower. She'd promised the girls they could finish it today if it had dried. Felisa spent a lot of time with the girls, and she would have thought Mrs. Drake would be grateful she took such good care of them. But the woman saw her as the enemy, trying to turn the twins against their nanny. From all Felisa could tell, the girls weren't fond of the nanny before Felisa had arrived.

With Juanita off for the day, Felisa had prepared breakfast, did the chores and, later in the afternoon, checked the new piñata. Confident it had dried, she settled the girls around the table to finish it. Once again they were covered with paste and strips of crepe paper, but the twins had so much fun it gave her joy to watch them.

Mrs. Drake had come by, complaining about their noise and asked how the twins could benefit from making the colorful Mexican toy. Felisa kept calm and told the woman the girls were having fun and that was important. Mrs. Drake had lifted her nose and strutted away, mumbling under her breath.

When the pretty flower piñata had been strung up again to dry, Felisa looked at her watch and decided to clean the mess later. She headed into the kitchen to prepare dinner. Without Juanita, the family was at her mercy for meals. She loved the comfortable kitchen with its wide space and cooking gadgets, a microwave oven, and a refrigerator that actually spit ice cubes from the door. She could only shake her head at the amazing things she'd seen since she came to the Garrison household.

A noise sounded in the yard, and she looked out the window. When Chad walked from the garage and lowered the door, then turned to the girls, happiness filled her. She couldn't resist being part of the greeting, so she lifted Nate in his carrier and followed the girls' chatter to the patio.

"Look, Daddy," Joy said, tugging at her father's arm as she pointed to the piñata hanging from a beam of the portico.

Felisa watched him, looking at their handiwork with pride.

"Wow! You decorated that all by yourselves?"

Joy crinkled her nose. "Felisa helped us."

"But they did most of it," she said. "I just cut out the flower petals."

"I've never seen such a pretty posy," Chad said, opening his arms to the girls.

They rushed in for a big hug and wrapped their arms around his neck while he lifted both of them into the air.

"You girls are getting too heavy," he said, lowering them to the ground. "I'll break my back."

"Pick up Felisa," Faith said. "She didn't get a hug."

"No, she didn't," he said, giving Felisa a grin.

"It was nothing," Felisa said, waving his words away while her pulse tripped through her. "I'd better get inside and fix dinner."

"Give her a hug, Daddy," Joy coaxed, as she maneuvered behind him and pushed him toward Felisa.

Felisa stepped back, her mind whirring while her heart thundered in her ears.

Chad stepped closer and opened his arms, then drew her into them, his manly scent filling her senses. Felisa prayed he couldn't feel her heart hammering against his broad chest. His gaze met hers, a hint of surprise and a glint of pleasure.

A sound came from over his shoulder, and as Chad released her, Felisa leaned around to see Mrs. Drake standing just outside the door beneath the portico. The woman spun around and marched inside the house.

Chad's cheery expression faded to dismay. "I'm sorry," he said.

As if a cold rain had covered the sunshine and dampened their spirits, Felisa felt a chill reel up her back as she watched Chad stride toward the house.

"Girls," she said, wanting to keep them away from the confrontation, "let's clean this table, please. It's going to be dinnertime soon."

Their attention hadn't left the back door, but she clapped her hands and waved toward the mess of newspaper covered with colorful markers, bottles of glue, and leftover strips of crepe paper, its color soaking into the damp paper beneath. As they worked she eyed the door, hoping for Chad to return; but he didn't, and the worry darkened her mood.

"Can we go inside?" Joy asked, as if aware something bad had happened.

"I thought you'd like to help me diaper Nate and get him ready for bed so I can finish dinner." She'd never let the girls help her before, but they'd become gentle with him, and today it seemed a necessity to distract them from their curiosity about Mrs. Drake.

"Can we really?" Faith asked.

"Really," she said, shoving the paper and scraps into a trash can they'd brought from the garage. "You can leave the other things on the table for now."

Her ploy worked. They skipped beside her to her quarters, pulled from the issues going on inside, but Felisa couldn't keep her mind from drifting there. What did Mrs. Drake think? The possibilities filled Felisa's mind and made her flinch.

With a dry diaper and his sleepers on, Nate flailed his arms and jammed his fist into his mouth. Felisa prayed the trouble in the house had ended, because she needed to send the girls on their way and finish dinner. Before she had to make the decision, she heard a rap on the door and raised her head. Chad stood outside, waiting.

"Let your daddy in," she said.

Joy darted to the door and flung the screen open. "Want to see Nate ready for bed?"

"I sure do," he said, "and guess what? You can go and play now until dinner, and bed's early tonight. We have church tomorrow."

Church. Memories of her family's church in Guadalajara filled Felisa's mind. The arched ceiling covered by a beautiful mural, the statues, the candles, and the hard wooden pews where she knelt in prayer. Although she'd been born and raised in that church, she'd always left the service knowing she was a sinner who needed prayers and intercessions for her evil ways.

She'd wondered about Chad's church since she'd arrived. When he came home from worship, he walked through the door whistling a song that seemed so joyful it made her heart ache with the longing to feel that same way. She'd asked Juanita about the song, and she'd said it was a praise hymn. She'd never heard a praise hymn in Guadalajara, at least not one that made her feel like that.

Chad clapped his hands as if shooing the girls out the door like chickens. "Go inside now. We'll be there in a minute."

"Oh, pooey," Faith said.

Chad tapped her on the head. "What's this I hear? After all that fun with Felisa helping you make a piñata, you're going to whine?"

Faith lowered her head. "I'm sorry."

Chad bent down and kissed her cheek, then kissed Joy's.

The girls gave the baby a quick kiss on the cheek; then, to Felisa's surprise, Joy kissed her, too. Not to be outdone, Faith did the same and added a hug. Felisa couldn't help but laugh when Joy returned to give her a hug, too.

"Competition," she said when they'd scampered out the door. She rose from the bed and carried Nate to the crib, then turned on the intercom so she'd hear him in the kitchen.

"In more ways than one," he said, his face losing the smile he'd had for the girls. Felisa knew he was referring to Mrs. Drake.

"What happened?"

He shook his head. "It's not your problem."

She tucked the blanket around Nate, then turned to him. "It is my problem if I caused it."

"You didn't cause any problem. I wasn't aware that she. . . ."

"Mrs. Drake?"

He nodded. "Don't worry. She feels very threatened by you and for good reason."

Felisa's back stiffened. "Threatened?" She studied his face. "I've done everything trying to make friends with her. She won't let me."

"She's jealous and prejudiced."

"Prejudiced because I'm Hispanic?" Felisa studied his face.

"Yes, and envious of your time with the twins."

"But she could do things with them, too." Then she thought about what had happened and stepped closer to Chad. Her heart beat in her throat. "She saw me in your arms, didn't she? What did she say?"

He shook his head again. "Nothing that holds any truth."

Felisa realized the time had come to talk. "I should leave. Nate is so healthy, and he's small. I can carry him in a sling on my back with no problem. I'll return to the fields on Monday."

Chad clasped her forearms in each hand. "Who will be the girls' nanny if you leave?"

"I'm used to field work. I've—" His words swung through her mind, then struck her. "What do you mean?"

"Mrs. Drake has threatened to quit numerous times. This time I took her up on the offer. She'll be leaving tomorrow. You can't leave now."

"But—"

His grip softened, and he drew her closer. "I told you earlier today, Felisa, that you've brought joy back into our lives. You've helped me see what the girls need. They need a father who gives them time and attention. Your care for the girls has done wonders. They've changed in the short time you've been here."

"Children need love and caring. . .as well as discipline. That was Mrs. Drake's mistake."

"I see that now," he said.

She felt him quiver. Chad lowered his face toward hers, his eyes hooded, and her chest tightened with anticipation. She waited for the kiss—a kiss she should refuse, but one she wanted so badly.

"Will you stay, Felisa? Please," Chad said, his voice husky and so near—until he bolted backward.

His action startled her, and the tender words left her disappointed yet grateful he'd behaved wisely in his self-control. He could promise her nothing, and she respected that he wouldn't toy with her heart.

"I'll stay until you find someone else."

"Someone else?" His eyes pleaded with her.

"It's best."

"I will find someone else to help Juanita, but I can't replace you."

She held her breath and sent up a prayer, trying to make a wise decision.

"You can have Mrs. Drake's room if you'd like, and I can put the—"

"No. I love my room. It's off the courtyard, and I can see the sun and hear the fountain and—" She swallowed, realizing she'd already answered his request.

"Then you can keep your room. Anything." He studied her face then touched her shoulder. "Will you go to church with us in the morning?"

"Church?" His invitation whirled through her. The vision of his spirit-filled face, the remembrance of the joyful hymn he often whistled, grasped her curiosity. "Is it wise?"

"Mrs. Drake often went with us."

"As their nanny?"

He studied her a moment. "Yes, as their nanny."

"I'll go to worship with you then, and thank you for inviting me." She braced herself against the sensation that rolled up her back. Stand guard, she told herself, then sent up a prayer. *Lord, help me walk the path You've prepared for me. That's all I ask.*

seven

Felisa stepped inside the church building, her focus jumping from one side of the huge space to the other. She viewed the comfortable seats, the large windows looking out to a garden on one side and the mountains on the other, and a vestibule that brought the outdoors in with large potted plants and light colored woods.

"Look at the church," she whispered in Nate's ear. She hadn't set foot in a church since his birth, and she felt ashamed. Her gaze drifted to the unusual setting—no statues, no vigil candles, no hard pews or tall stained-glass windows. Instead of an altar she saw a raised area where musicians assembled on one side and a group of singers formed on the other. A large screen hung from the center of the ceiling, and her head spun with questions. This was so different from the usual church she attended.

"You're frowning," Chad said, catching her off guard.

"I'm just looking around. I've never seen a church like this before."

A warm grin spread across his face. "Wait until you hear the music. You've never heard anything like it before, either."

Eyeing the band, she guessed Chad was right. An organ or sometimes guitars were what she'd sung to in church.

Felisa held Nate against her chest and followed Chad down the center aisle. About midway, he motioned her to turn into the row, and she shifted down a few seats with the girls after her, and then Chad. As soon as they were seated, the girls opened bags they'd picked up in the vestibule. Each sack was filled with crayons, coloring-book pictures of Jesus, and small toys, all kinds of delights to keep children quiet. Felisa chuckled at her feeble attempt. She'd dropped a few hard candies into her bag, thinking if the girls became restless, she could offer them a treat.

People streamed into the space, filling the seats as the musicians began to play a song she'd never heard but one that lifted her spirit. Some people clapped to the rhythm while others swayed. She bounced Nate in her arms to the beat of the music.

Soon a light flashed across the screen, and words appeared. A small group gathered near the front, the band grew louder, and the people rose, singing the words that continued to change above her head. Felisa didn't know the tune, but it was simple. Chad's deep rich baritone drifted over her. She envisioned the times he'd come home from church on Sunday, whistling a happy tune. Today she understood why. Joyous voices filled the air, and people lifted their arms toward heaven as if speaking to God. "We praise His holy name." The words soared through her mind, and Felisa recalled these past weeks when she'd praised God in her own quiet way.

The jubilant sound lifted her, and she felt a smile spread on her face, then tears well in her eyes. Tears of joy for God's blessings, tears of sorrow for her past, tears of uncertainty for what the future might hold, and tears of wonder at what God could provide. She glanced at the twins, who were standing on the seats, clapping their hands and singing the simple tune. Her heart filled with pure happiness. Joy beyond measure. She'd heard the phrase. Today she felt that joy permeating her body.

Finally the music resolved, and she settled into the comfortable seat to listen to the prayers and Bible readings. Nate seemed as mesmerized as she was by the happy songs.

A young man, dressed in a suit, stepped to the stand, and the people hushed. His strong voice warmed the room with his message of hope in Jesus. His words settled in Felisa's mind like a glorious rainbow. She'd trusted God, even when things were darkest, and He'd sent her a spectrum of color into her life—her beautiful son, the lovely home, Chad's friendship, and the love of two little impish girls.

The preacher, so different without a cleric's robe, captured Felisa with words she needed to hear. God loved her, He walked beside her each day, and He guided her steps. Guidance was what she needed so badly, God's wisdom and direction. The preacher opened the Bible and began to read from a psalm. *"Let the morning bring me word of your unfailing love, for I have put my trust in you. Show me the way I should go, for to you I lift up my soul."*

"Show me the way I should go, for to you I lift up my soul." She wanted to remember the verse so it would calm her when fears filled her mind and decisions spun in her head like water down a drain. Nate squirmed, and she lifted him higher and kissed his soft cheek. He smelled of powder and baby soap.

Thank You, Jesus, for this gift. She admired her son, then turned her gaze to Chad, whose eyes focused on her. She smiled, and when he winked she felt a flush warm her cheeks. He gave her a hand signal that he'd like to hold Nate, and she kissed her son's cheek, then handed him over to Chad. She watched him cuddle the baby against his broad chest, her son looking so tiny in his arms. Warmth fluttered in her chest, and she pressed her fingers against the spot to calm herself.

Joy wiggled beside her, and she gazed down at the girls, who had turned their attention to Nate in their father's arms. Her heart gave a tug. She would miss them terribly when she had to move away—and she would one day when Chad found a new nanny.

Nanny. A chill rolled down Felisa's back. She'd been uncomfortable with Mrs. Drake around and even more so yesterday when she'd threatened to quit and Chad had taken her up on her threat. At breakfast the woman's eyes were filled with anger. Felisa had decided to eat toast in her room and not endure the woman's silent contempt. Today was to be Mrs. Drake's last day, and she hoped the woman would be gone by the time they returned home from church. Felisa thanked the Lord, not for herself, but for the twins. They needed someone who loved them.

People rose around her, and Felisa was startled that the service was ending. She'd drifted off in her own thoughts, and she asked God to forgive her. The final hymn stirred Felisa most of all because it was the familiar tune Chad often whistled—"Lord, we lift Your name on high." When the service ended, she would be sure to thank Chad for inviting her to join them. She'd missed attending worship, and though this was so unlike her usual tradition, she loved the fellowship and the happiness that filled the air and her spirit.

⁂

Chad pulled into the drive and nosed the car toward the garage. He paused when he saw Mrs. Drake outside, loading her belongings into her trunk. She turned to look at them, her nose raised in a tilt that told him her thoughts.

"You can get out here if you'd like," he said, noticing Felisa's discomfort. "Girls, you can climb out, too. I want to talk with Mrs. Drake for a few moments, and then you can say good-bye."

"I don't want to," Faith said, her old belligerent attitude permeating her words.

"Faith," Chad said, giving her his get-ready-for-a-lecture look.

She lowered her head. "But—"

"Jesus said to be nice to people," Joy said, her motherly tone making Chad grin.

Faith gave her an elbow. "That's not in the Bible."

"Yes, it is," Chad said. "Love your neighbor as yourself."

Faith put her hands on her hips. "But she's not our neighbor."

"Everyone's your neighbor, Faith. We should treat people like we want to be treated even if they don't treat us nicely."

She sat for a moment as if she couldn't get a grip on the idea.

"You know the Golden Rule," Chad said. " 'Do unto others as you would have them do to you.' That means just about the same thing."

"Okay," Faith said, her voice not totally convincing.

Chad looked up and noticed that Felisa had already vanished inside her room with Nate. Joy stood by the car door, and Faith finally climbed out and shut it. The girls hurried off for the house, and Chad squared his shoulders, gathering his thoughts, then pulled into the garage.

"Can I help you, Mrs. Drake?" he said, as he stepped out.

"No, thank you." She didn't look his way.

"I have your check." He patted his pocket, glad he'd thought to get it ready. He handed it to her, and she studied it as if calculating for accuracy.

She tucked the check in her pocket, seeming to be satisfied, but she didn't mention the bonus he'd given her.

"I'm sorry you haven't been happy here, Mrs. Drake."

"I was fine until. . ."—she tilted her shoulder toward Felisa's doorway—"until she came along, trying to stir up trouble."

"Felisa didn't stir up any problems. I told you that the other day. She's been very good with the girls. They like her, and—"

"And so do you," she said, her eyes narrowed, "too much,

and you call her Felisa. What about Mrs. Carrillo, or did you forget she's married? I find it disgusting."

He drew back from her biting words. "She's a widow." He was stunned by her insinuation. "Nothing inappropriate has gone on in this house, Mrs. Drake. I hope you don't—"

"God sits in judgment, Mr. Garrison. I don't."

She was judging him, and wrongly so. "I think your decision to leave is a good one. You're obviously bitter and prejudiced, and—"

"Prejudiced!" She straightened her back like a flagpole. "Facts are facts. You just don't know the truth."

A scowl weighted his brows, and he stared at the woman, trying to makes sense out of her words. "What truth?"

"Never mind." She waved him away. "I'm nearly finished here; then you can wallow in your delusion."

He jammed his fists into his pockets. "Truth? Delusion? You're making no sense."

"I've heard her talk. Look around you, Mr. Garrison. This woman came from an impoverished background. No education. No social skills. Can't you see she's using you? She's after your money and a green card. She's come out and said it."

Green card? What was she talking about? "Felisa has a green card, Mrs. Drake."

"That's what she's told you." She slammed her trunk lid and turned on him. "If you want that kind of lying woman to influence your little girls, that's your sin. I pity you, Mr. Garrison. Lust is a sin, you know."

He heard the door bang and saw the girls heading his way, but the woman didn't wait for the twins or his response. She climbed into her car, slammed her door, then revved the motor and backed from the garage.

Chad held up his hand to hold the twins back from getting run over by the irate woman. He watched her tear off, his heart thundering from her anger and from the sharp words she'd tossed in his face. Could there be some truth to her words? His heart said no, but reality said it was possible. He'd heard horror stories of men and women being duped into falling in love and marrying someone only to learn the love was for money or prestige, but Felisa would never do that to him.

"Where'd she go?" Joy asked, hurrying to him as Mrs. Drake vanished down the driveway and around the corner of the house.

"I guess she had to rush," he said, dazed by the incident and the look of bewilderment on the girls' faces.

"Can we play?" Faith asked, a smile growing on her face.

"Sure. Until lunch."

They skipped off, and he stood looking at the rolling foothills with his heart in his throat. He lived in a lovely setting, amid God's glorious bounty of trees, mountains, and fresh air. He turned and faced his expansive home—the fountain's soft tinkle, the coral stucco and tile roof that offered not only a shelter but luxury, as well.

Felisa had, at times, lived in her car. His gaze shifted to the doorway to her room. Inside, he guessed she was feeding Nate, perhaps sitting on the queen-size bed in the well-appointed room. She'd said she'd never seen so much space. She told him once she'd never taken a real bubble bath until she'd come here. He'd had women give him the come-on look after Janie died, and he'd never given one a thought until Felisa. What had drawn her to him?

He needed to think. He knew Mrs. Drake spoke out of anger, and anger didn't always carry truth. Yet he felt like a jury who heard testimony before the judge told them to disregard it. Once a juror heard the witness, how could he forget what he'd heard? He closed his eyes for a moment, letting the sun warm the chill that ran down his back. His feet felt glued to the ground, his stomach knotted, and his breath constricted. He raised his eyes to heaven, gulping at the air, until the feeling passed.

"Lord, You know the truth," he whispered. "It's in Your hands."

❧

Monday morning Felisa struggled to concentrate. She sensed something had happened before Mrs. Drake had left. Chad had seemed quiet at dinner, except to tell her he'd hired a young woman to help Juanita. She hoped this one was gentler than Mrs. Drake. The girls had mentioned the nanny had gone without a good-bye to them. Felisa wasn't sure if it made the twins sad or relieved.

She'd eyed Chad as they ate, wondering if he regretted the woman's quitting her job or if something else had set him on edge. After dinner he slipped away without making eye contact, and Felisa lingered at the table, trying to make sense out of it.

Had she done something to offend him? Her mind dug back into the past day, but nothing came to mind. She'd thanked him for inviting her to the worship service. She'd truly felt blessed by being there. She'd taken good care of the girls when he stopped to chat with people he knew.

The image tightened in her head. Had someone made a comment about her? She cowered beneath the thought, knowing she didn't fit into Chad's world even as a nanny.

Yet she thought back to their trip home from church when she and Chad had talked as if nothing was wrong. They'd laughed, and she'd mentioned hearing him come home from previous worship services whistling the praise song they'd sung and how it made her feel good inside. He'd given her shoulder a squeeze and said how glad he felt that she enjoyed the service.

She pictured him in church with Nate in his arms. His face had glowed when he held her son, and again the sting of fear rippled to her stomach and churned the small amount of breakfast she'd forced herself to eat. Though she'd tried to push the fear aside, sometimes she imagined that Chad had manipulated the situation to get his hands on her son. The thought slid across her like ice, chilling her to the bone.

Finally she rose and carried her plate and silverware into the kitchen. She scraped and rinsed the dishes and utensils while Juanita loaded the dishwasher.

"You're quiet today."

Juanita's voice startled her, and she jumped.

"Aren't you feeling well?" Juanita asked. "Maybe you had too much sun this weekend."

"No, I'm fine."

Juanita's eyes narrowed as she searched her face. "You're not fine."

Unable to hide anything from Juanita's sharp eyes, she gave a nod. "I'm curious, I guess."

"Curious? I thought you might be upset about Mrs. Drake's leaving."

Felisa's chest constricted. "Why would I be upset?"

"She blames you. I thought you knew that."

"Cha—" She caught herself. "Mr. Garrison said she was jealous that the girls liked me."

Juanita raised her brows, then nodded. "I'm sure that's part of it."

Part of it? What did that mean? She turned toward Juanita but found her heading away. Felisa stood beside the sink with questions roiling in her head.

Juanita returned with the dust mop and dragged it across the floor, never looking up.

Though she wanted to ask, she hesitated. Juanita didn't

gossip, and she could get very close mouthed when pressed. Instead Felisa made use of the time to ask the lingering question that had often troubled her. "Why is Mr. Garrison so interested in Nate?" She'd been more careful this time to say *Mr. Garrison*. Her slip had been careless.

Juanita paused and leaned against the dust mop. "He's a kind man, and he likes children."

"But I think it's more than that. He's always wanting to hold Nate and—"

"He has his reasons, but it's his business. It's not my way to gossip about my employer. I hope you understand, Felisa," she said kindly. "He'll tell you if he wants to."

She gave the mop a long push and delved into her task, leaving Felisa with questions dangling in her thoughts but no one to ask. Juanita had made it clear that she'd said enough.

❧

For a week, uneasiness had weighed on Chad's shoulders. When he looked at Felisa, he saw her questioning, sad eyes. She clung to Nate when he was nearby as if he were an ogre who planned to steal her child. He made no sense out of that; yet he understood her concern. She must have sensed his wariness.

The new girl was working out. Gloria liked the twins and related to Juanita well. Juanita said she was a hard worker and seemed trustworthy. Chad had talked to the pastor before hiring the young woman. She'd recently joined the church and she'd had some personal problems; but the pastor vouched for her, and that was all Chad needed.

On Saturday he took the girls into Salinas to pick up some paperwork he'd left behind in his office. His mind had been everywhere but on his job, and he promised them a trip to a fast-food restaurant where they could play on the plastic slides and tubes, then burrow into the huge mound of colorful plastic balls. They had begged to go there, but he'd avoided it. Greasy food and screaming kids weren't his idea of a relaxing lunch, but he'd finally given in. He needed to spend time with the twins, and at home Felisa was always around. Today he left Felisa behind, and he saw her study him with a question.

They'd spoken to each other during the week, but the conversation was strained. He kept his distance. He'd nearly lost his heart. Since Mrs. Drake's charges against her he'd thought back, trying to find the clues to Felisa's intentions that he might have missed. Mrs. Drake's accusation made little sense when he thought about it. He'd been the one to insist on taking Felisa to the hospital. She'd begged him not to. He'd been the one who had given her the housekeeper job. She'd had no idea of his plans. So if he'd been the one to arrange her stay at the house, when had her goal to trick him been devised?

Chad sat at the small, round table, watching the girls through the restaurant window, and rubbed his temples. He missed his conversations with Felisa. He missed holding Nate, who seemed to grow an inch each day. His dark hair had already grown thick and curly like Felisa's. The boy followed motion with his deep brown eyes. He would be smart like his mother.

His thoughts shifted. Chad knew nothing of Felisa's husband except that he'd been run down by a passing car. He assumed her life had been hard. Migrant workers had to be strong people who could deal with moving from place to place, living in low-income housing, and working in the draining heat of the day. Felisa had stamina. She'd handled the girls with patience and taken over the housekeeping job with skill, and he'd found her to be an excellent cook.

Besides her homemaking skills, Felisa was a beautiful woman with strength of character. He'd come to think of her as honest and trustworthy, a woman of faith. She'd never asked for anything special. Even the day he planned to take them all to the beach, she had assumed he meant only the girls. That didn't sound like a woman on the make to him. He trusted Juanita, and she seemed to like Felisa.

Juanita. Why hadn't she warned him if she'd sensed something awry? She had given him odd looks the past few days, but she'd probably noticed his distraction. Juanita had never been a gossip. She'd always been one to avoid rumors. Still, he couldn't believe Juanita would be aware of Felisa's attempts to manipulate him into marriage and not say something.

Rumors. Gossip. Juanita followed God's Word. The Bible said to slander no one. Had Juanita not told him about Felisa's motives because she thought it wrong to spread rumors? Chad's thoughts wavered in one direction and then another.

His head pounded while Bible verses raced through his mind. A verse from Proverbs struck him. *"He who conceals his hatred has lying lips, and whoever spreads slander is a fool."* He needed to question Juanita. Mrs. Drake had probably been lying. Juanita would tell him the truth if he asked her.

Chad rose and wandered to the door and out into the play area. He stood looking into the tubes and plastic pathways, smiling at his daughters as they waved and called to him. They had become happy children. He'd become a more light-hearted man, a man who could feel again and see a brighter future. How could he think Felisa had plotted to harm him and his family? She'd been a blessing, a gift from the Lord. How could he doubt her?

eight

Felisa sat outside her room, nestling Nate against her and listening to the quiet. The only sound was the splash of the fountain and an occasional birdcall. She'd weighed her thoughts carefully, and though she still had no idea what had disturbed Chad, she sensed his interest in Nate was from his heart and nothing more.

Chad seemed too tender and too loving to want to take her little boy from her. She winced at the evil thought that had settled into her mind. Chad, a Christian through and through, would no more hurt her than he would hurt Joy or Faith. A chill of loneliness settled over her. Usually she would have gone with Chad to tend to the girls, but today he'd not invited her. She still struggled to recall what she might have done to offend him.

Being the nanny seemed almost a waste of time. She'd been close to the girls before when Mrs. Drake was nanny and she still did chores around the house. Now Gloria had been hired to help Juanita, and Felisa could spend more time with Nate; but she also had more time to think and to brood. The happiness she'd felt for the past weeks had faded like a wilting rose.

Glancing down, she noticed Nate had drifted to sleep. She rose, carried him to his crib, and placed him down for a nap, then set the monitor in case she went inside the house for some reason. From her chair outside, she could hear his cry. She closed the screen door softly and settled again on the chair in the warm sunlight, trying to recapture the contentment she'd felt until the past week.

The crunch of automobile tires sounded around the corner of the house, and she looked up to see Chad's dark-blue sedan pull in front of the garage as the door opened. The girls scampered out, each carrying a package. They darted toward her, and her loneliness dissipated.

"Did you have fun?" she asked.

Joy nodded while Faith opened her parcel and pulled out a box. "Look what Daddy bought me."

When Chad's shadow fell at Felisa's feet, she glanced up. His sad eyes glided over her before he walked away into the house.

"Aren't you going to look at my present?" Faith asked, holding the box in front of her.

She pulled her gaze from Chad's retreating back and forced a smile. "Let me see."

Faith opened the box and pulled out wind chimes attached to a brightly painted metal sunflower. "Listen." She held the flower in the air, letting the metal pieces tinkle as they struck one another.

"It's beautiful," Felisa said. "We can hang it on the edge of the portico so it will be stirred by the breeze."

"Will you help me hang it?" she asked.

"We'll need a hammer and nails." Felisa paused. "Maybe your daddy can hang it better. He's taller."

"Okay," she said, skipping off while Joy stood beside her holding her little box in her hands.

"Do you want to see my present?"

"I do," Felisa said, realizing from Joy's expression she felt left out. "What do you have?"

Joy lifted the lid on the box and pulled back the paper. "It's a butterfly."

The colorful metal butterfly with moveable wings hung

from a lightweight cord, and though it wouldn't clang, it would certainly sway in the breeze. "I love it, Joy. It's so beautiful."

"Like you," the little girl said, wrenching Felisa's heart.

"Thank you. That's the sweetest thing to say." She held the cord and watched the butterfly flutter on the light breeze. "Is this for your room?"

She shook her head. "It's for outside."

Felisa placed the butterfly back into the box and handed it to Joy. "Your daddy can help you hang this, too."

Joy held the box against her chest and stared at the ground, her toe bouncing from side to side on the patio tiles.

Felisa studied her face. "Is something wrong?"

She shook her head without looking up.

"Did you get into trouble today?"

Joy shook her head again.

"Then why are you so sad?" She tilted her chin upward. "Can I help?"

Joy nodded. "I want you to be my mommy."

Felisa's heart spiraled to her throat and back. "Oh, Joy." She wrapped her arms around the girl. "I'm your nanny. Isn't that almost as good?"

"But someday you'll leave, and then I won't have you anymore." She searched Felisa's eyes, and Joy's expression clasped her heart and twisted it.

She couldn't promise the child she would never leave, because she knew she would. Words clung to her throat. "I'm so honored that you love me so much, Joy. Thank you. I love you, too. Very, very much."

"Then you could be my mommy." Her eyelashes fluttered, and she gave Felisa a questioning look. "I don't remember my real mommy. I was too little."

"I'm sure she loved you very much." Felisa knew that if Joy were her child she would have indeed loved her with all of her being. She held the child closer, wondering why this troubled Joy now. Was it Mrs. Drake's leaving? The child had lost a mother and many nannies. Felisa ached, thinking of the pain she would cause this little girl when she had to go.

She heard the door slam and looked toward the sound. Faith had already cajoled her father into hanging the wind chime. He stood beneath a crossbeam at the edge of the portico, holding the hammer and apparently searching for a place to hang the chime where it would best catch the wind.

She gave Joy a pat. "You'd better get over there so he can hang your butterfly."

Joy rallied and skipped away with her small box clutched in her hands.

Felisa stayed in the chair and watched from a distance. Normally she would have been with the girls, helping decide where the chime should go, but the past days she felt as if she were an outsider.

Chad looked her way, then went back to work, pounding a nail into the wooden beam and hanging the chime. He moved closer to her side of the patio and hung Joy's butterfly. When he stepped away, the lovely creature dipped and fluttered, just as Felisa's heart had done for so long.

He headed back to the house with the girls, and she settled back and closed her eyes. She hated to face dinner, and her mind worked to find a reason why she wouldn't eat at all or would eat in her room. She didn't want to lie, but she just couldn't face him any longer.

"Felisa."

His soft, raspy voice rippled past her ear. She opened her eyes to see Chad standing above her.

"I'm sorry to disturb you," he said, "but I think we should talk."

She shook her head, wondering if she'd fallen asleep and this was only a dream or if it were real. She watched his serious face flicker with emotion and tried to read the meaning. He was letting her go back to the fields as she'd requested. "Talk? You mean—"

"I owe you an apology."

"Apology?" Felisa had never been so surprised.

He gave a fleeting nod. "For my behavior."

She lowered her gaze, watching the shadows from his body shift over her. He'd acted strangely—distant, really—but then so had she. "I—I know I did something wrong, and I've wanted to apologize to you."

"What do you mean you did something wrong?"

She rose, feeling uncomfortable sitting while he stood. "I must have. You've been upset with me."

"What did you do?"

She searched his face. "You tell me, because I don't know."

The stern look cracked into a faint grin. "You did nothing wrong, Felisa. It was me. I listened to rumors and—"

"Rumors?"

"Gossip. Mrs. Drake told me. . ." He motioned to the umbrella table. "Let me get a chair so we can really talk."

She watched him move across the tile surface of the patio, lift the chair, and carry it to her side. When he returned, she sank back into her seat, the muscles of her legs feeling empty of strength. Felisa folded her hands in her lap and waited to learn what Mrs. Drake had told him. She'd rarely spoken to the woman.

Chad leaned forward, resting his elbows on his knees, his hands fidgeting in front of him until he wove his fingers together. He raised his head, his eyes searching hers as if he were struggling to find the words to say. "The Bible tells us not to listen to hearsay, not to spread false rumors, and I failed miserably."

His expression made her ache. "I don't understand."

"I'm ashamed to tell you what I gave credence to."

"Credence?" She didn't know what the word meant.

"What I thought might be a possibility."

"Maybe it doesn't matter." She lowered her gaze and shook her head.

He leaned closer, capturing her hand in his. "It does matter, Felisa. It matters a great deal, because I should know you better. I should have trusted you."

The warmth of his flesh heated her skin and sent electricity surging up her arm. Her mind swirled with his words and her lack of understanding, while her breath seemed to leave her. What had Mrs. Drake said, and why hadn't he told her?

"Mrs. Drake hired on as my third nanny in less than two years. I wanted to give her a chance. God tells us not to judge, and though I thought she was a controlling woman, I gave her time to get to know the twins and to ease up on them. I wanted her to love the girls, but—"

"Seeing the truth isn't judging. I'm sure your instinct told you the twins were unhappy."

"Yes, but so was I, and sometimes I couldn't sort out the difference. All kids hate being disciplined. I figured. . ." He brushed away his words. "Never mind that. When I talked with her as she was leaving, she became vicious. Her anger said things about you that I don't even want to think about. I finally spoke to Juanita. She would know if there were any truth in what Mrs. Drake said, and—"

"What things? What did she say?" Her nerves chafed with the waiting.

"That you were plotting for me to fall in love so you could get to my money and a green card."

The words knifed through her. She shook her head, unable to form the idea in her mind. The reality sank deeper and embedded into her brain. "Money? Green card? I told you I had a green card."

"I know," he said with a look that made her ache for him. "I knew you had a green card, but—"

Tears blurred her eyes and rolled down her cheeks. Why deny it? Some Americans—gringos, as her fellow workers called them—would think something this awful about her. She knew she didn't even fit into his world as a nanny.

"Please, Felisa," he said, rising and crouching beside her, his arms slipping around her shoulders and drawing her to him. "Please. I didn't believe it, but it made me question. She'd said you told her this. My heart said no, but my head said. . ."

His words faded away, and all she could hear was the beating of her heart and his deep breathing. His scent encircled her, a fresh, earthy aroma like lemons in a spring rain. She felt the stubble of his jaw against her forehead and his fingers caressing her arms. Ashamed and amazed, she lifted her head, not wanting to pull away but knowing she must.

"I'm sorry for crying. I—"

He looked into her face and wiped the tears from her cheeks with his finger. "I didn't mean to hurt you. I'm so sorry. All the things I've said to you—how you've changed our lives and made us happy again—all of those things I meant from the bottom of my heart. My daughters adore you. I ado—" He halted. "I can never express how I feel about your effect on this house. As I said, you made it a home again."

Sadness washed over her. Chad's wife had died, and he'd raised two little girls alone. She would have to raise Nate alone. Her son filled her thoughts—his sweet face and tiny limbs, but raising him alone seemed different. She'd sensed that Chad had loved his wife far more than she'd loved her husband. His sorrow had to be as deep as an abyss. Without thinking, she touched his face, her fingers tracing his unshaven face. His firm jaw jerked beneath her hand, his eyes searched hers.

"You don't have to apologize," she said. "I understand. We all have fears that scare us like a snake hiding in the grass, its tail giving us warning, but we can't believe what we hear."

He pressed his hand against hers, flooding her with warmth. The pressure deepened the scratch of his whiskers, reminding her that life could be a mixture of pleasure and pain. Her heart wanted to love him, but her wisdom told her to beware.

Felisa drew in a ragged breath, a shiver coursing through her body.

Chad released her hand, his eyes saying more than her reasoning could accept. He rose and looked into the distance. She followed his gaze to the purple haze of the mountains, the blue-green of the thick growth of trees clinging to their sides, standing tall and straight as if God were holding them with a wire.

She tried to stand, but her legs trembled erratically. What had happened? What had been the meaning of the intimate moment they'd shared? Hearing a soft cry from her room, she grasped her courage and rose. "Nate," she said, her voice almost a whisper.

His tender smile filled her. "Can I come in? I've missed him."

She nodded, aware that she, too, had had her bad thoughts about him. She needed to confess her fear that he wanted to steal her son. Sadness bounded through her as she admitted to herself what she'd thought.

Inside, Felisa lifted Nate from his crib. He quieted as she kissed his warm cheek. "Hold him while I get a clean diaper," she said, handing him to Chad.

Chad opened his arms and cuddled her son to his chest, while she dug into a drawer for Nate's clean clothes. When she returned, Chad placed Nate on the bed. "May I?"

She eyed him. "You want to change his diaper?"

"Why not?"

"It's dirty."

"That's okay."

She sat on the edge of the bed, watching as Chad removed the diaper, cleaned the baby, powdered him, and attached the new diaper. He reached for the blue one-piece body suit and drew it onto Nate's legs, fitted his arms into the sleeves, and snapped it closed. "There you go, big man," he said, kissing the top of her son's head. "You're as good-looking as your mother."

He cradled Nate in his arms, giving him a slow bounce as his gaze met hers. "Was his father a handsome man?"

His question addled her. "Yes."

"You don't sound convinced," he said, seeing too deeply into her emotions.

"He had a handsome face, but his soul wasn't handsome at all." She felt sad saying the truth.

His expression darkened. "Why did you marry him?"

"Stupidity." She shook her head. "I was young and inexperienced. He was handsome and promised many things. It sounded better than the crowded conditions of my family, and. . .I knew it would be a relief to my parents. One less person underfoot, one less mouth to feed. You understand."

"So you married to make life easier for your family?"

She drew up her shoulders. "I was sixteen. I'm not sure I thought of it that way. I felt a burden to my parents. I wanted to go to school, but they wanted me to work. I thought of it as an escape."

He gave her a nod and studied her. "I'm sorry. Life hasn't been easy for you."

"But it's made me strong."

A telling look stole across his face. "Yes, you are strong."

He placed his hand on her shoulder and drew her closer as her pulse tripped along her limbs and thundered in her temples. She saw his lips twitch, and he leaned closer, their gazes locked, words unspoken.

A breeze must have set the wind chimes to swaying, because Felisa heard a soft tinkle. The distraction caused her to turn. Then footsteps sounded outside, and the girls' voices fluttered into the room. The girls, not a breeze, had touched the chimes, she realized as they arrived outside the door.

She'd been holding her breath, sensing something wonderful had nearly happened, but she released the pent-up stream of air.

Chad gave her an uneasy look and stepped back.

"What are you doing?" Joy asked, pressing her nose against the screen.

"Changing Nate's diaper," Chad said.

Faith's eyes widened. "Did you change it?"

"I did." He handed the baby to Felisa.

"It's almost dinnertime," Joy said.

Faith used her hands as blinders as she peered inside. "Juanita said come in five minutes."

Chad shot her a questioning look, and Felisa gave him a nod.

"I'd better get inside." He pushed against the screen and vanished with Faith and Joy chattering beside him, their voices fading with the distance.

Felisa sat on the edge of the bed, her throat tight with frustration. She was falling in love. She couldn't stop herself, and she would be so hurt. She nestled Nate against her, feeling the need to go somewhere. She needed to talk to someone who would listen and understand. She missed Maria, her coworker in the field. They used to talk about their troubles. She wondered if Maria even knew she and the baby were okay. Had anyone told her?

Tomorrow was Sunday. She would visit Maria. She could find her easily. She lived with her sister and brother in one of the low-income housing units. Maybe she would take Maria to lunch. That would be a treat for her friend, and the woman could see Nate. Yes. That's what she had to do.

She assumed Maria would be happy for her, but the more she thought about it the more the idea unsettled her. What if Maria gave her a hundred reasons why she should get out of the Garrison household? Would she listen? Felisa couldn't answer her own question.

nine

Felisa pulled onto the street and studied the houses. They all looked alike, and she hoped she could find Maria. Chad had seemed disappointed she drove her own car to church; but she explained her desire to visit Maria, and he understood. The twins had wanted to go with her, but that would have ended her purpose. She couldn't talk openly with Maria with the girls listening.

She'd enjoyed the service again today, but the more she listened and watched, the more questions arose. How could these worshippers be so joyful when God punished sinners? Why did they smile and raise their arms to heaven when she fell on her knees with downcast eyes for fear of God's anger? She related more to Chad's God than the God she'd known in Mexico, and it troubled her.

The familiar car outside the small house triggered Felisa's confidence. It belonged to Maria's brother. She would have called first if they had a phone. Felisa knew she would be disappointed if Maria wasn't home. She parked in front and climbed from the car.

She paused, looking toward the house and wondering if she should bother to unhook Nate from the carrier. But before she could move, the door flew open, and she heard Maria's voice.

"Felisa!" Her friend charged out the door, her arms open wide. "¡Hola!"

"¡Hola!" Felisa embraced her friend then pulled her toward the rear car door. "Come. Look," she said in Spanish, gesturing toward Nate.

"Your baby!" Maria cried in Spanish, clapping her hands then giving Felisa another hug. "Is it a girl or boy?"

"*Hijo*," Felisa said, letting her know she'd had a boy.

Felisa unlatched Nate from the car seat, still speaking in Spanish. "His name is Nataniel. I call him Nate."

"It's a beautiful name," Maria said, "and he's a beautiful boy. Does he look like Miguel?"

She gave a small shrug. "Chad says he looks like me."

Maria's eyes widened. "Chad?"

Felisa cringed, wishing she'd not called him by his first name. "Did you wonder where I've been?"

"I worried about you." She stood back and looked at her from head to toe. "But you look wonderful. Better than wonderful."

"I'm working for Mr. Garrison as a nanny."

"A nanny," Maria said, her face reflecting her surprise.

Felisa told her the story of her invitation to the Garrison home and how she'd worked as a housekeeper until the nanny left. She avoided telling Maria the reason for Mrs. Drake's leaving. Sharing the personal information wasn't her right.

"I'm happy for you, Felisa," Maria said, but Felisa heard envy in her voice and almost felt sorry she'd come to visit. She hadn't meant to make her friend jealous.

"I wish you could have this kind of gift from God," she said, deciding she'd said enough.

"I'm sure life is easier now without working the fields," Maria said, understanding what gift she meant.

Felisa only nodded and turned her attention to Nate. She'd come to ask Maria's opinion, but now the look in her friend's eyes made her have second thoughts.

"May I hold him?" Maria asked.

"Yes. Yes." Felisa bounced him lightly as she placed Nate into her friend's arms. "He's such a good baby."

Maria smiled. "I'm glad."

Felisa stood beside her, uncomfortable she'd come to see her. Her questions lodged in her throat, and she knew she couldn't ask them now. She would have to find the answers herself—between her and God—because she had no one else.

"Do you live nearby?"

"Nearby? No. I live in—" She faltered. "I live further out. I have a room."

"Good," Maria said. "I worried about you in your car. Will you come back to the fields?"

Felisa swallowed her discomfort. "One day, when Mr. Garrison finds a new nanny. The job is only temporary."

"That's too bad," Maria said, "but I'll look forward to seeing you in the fields again."

Felisa looked toward the sun, calculating the time. "I suppose I should be going. I just wanted to let you know Nate and I are doing fine."

Maria handed back Nate, then bit the edge of her lip. "I'm sorry not to invite you in. It's so crowded in—"

Felisa held up her hand. "No. That's okay, Maria. I understand. I only planned to stop for a minute." She buckled Nate back into his seat, then turned to Maria. "I'll see you one day again. I'm not sure when."

Maria opened her arms, and Felisa went into them, sharing an embrace. She stepped back and slid into her car. "*Hasta la vista*, Maria."

"*Adios.*"

She shifted into gear and pulled away, tears flooding her eyes. She'd meant well, but she'd blundered. Maria could never understand how she'd given her heart to a man so unreachable. *Father, I know my heart will break, and all I ask is that I do Your will.*

❧

Chad sat at the umbrella table, playing kids' dominos with

Faith and Joy. The tinkle of the wind chimes had set him in a melancholy state. Though he'd apologized and assumed Felisa had forgiven him, he still sensed her reticence. Maybe it would take time. He had to be patient.

"It's your turn, Daddy," Faith said, giving him a questioning look.

"Sorry," he said, placing his two pink dots against another two on the table. The dominos snaked across the round table in a nonsensical trail, about as ludicrous as his thoughts. Since Felisa had pulled away from church in her old clunker, he'd had a sense of loss. He feared she would leave him as she'd suggested—once he found a replacement nanny.

He watched Faith take her turn, and his mind drifted as Joy pondered her next move. Truly Chad had no intention of looking for another nanny. He wanted Felisa. He wanted her for a nanny and a housekeeper and. . . His chest constricted, and perspiration beaded above his lip. He wanted Felisa as his wife.

"Impossible." His voice startled him, and he shifted his focus to see both girls frowning at him.

"It's not impossible," Joy said. "I matched three blue dots with three blue dots. See?"

He gave them a feeble grin. "I was just thinking." About love. About a complete family. About—

Both girls giggled, and he studied his tiles, finding a match for his green dot.

Chad needed someone to talk with. Men didn't bare their souls, but he had the urge to talk about his feelings for Felisa to someone and thought of his best friend, Dallas Jones. Dallas was a Christian and might understand. But every time Chad had tried to contact Dallas, he'd lost courage, fearing Dallas would call him crazy or list the reasons why a relationship was hopeless, even impossible. Chad wanted hope and kept putting his trust in God's hands alone. Still, hearing a friend's supportive comments would give him assurance.

A car approached on the gravel drive, and he felt his hand twitch as he organized the tiles on the tray. He forced himself not to turn around.

"It's Felisa!" Joy shouted, glee filling her voice. She jumped from her chair and skipped across the patio toward the garage.

"Are we ending the game?" Chad asked, welcoming the break.

"No," Faith said, "we're not done yet."

But he felt done. Finished. Wiped out. He could hear Joy's chatter behind her and Felisa's voice greeting them. Felisa's heels tapped along the tiles as she approached.

"Having fun?" she asked, carrying Nate in the carrier.

"Yes!" both twins said at the same time.

"Sure thing," he said, giving her a look to know this wasn't his favorite Sunday-afternoon activity.

"Wanna play?" Joy asked, patting the arm of the fourth chair.

She shook her head. "I'm a little late to get in now. Anyway I have to feed Nate."

Chad studied her, seeing the sun highlighting her dark hair, her cheeks tanned and rosy, and her summer dress as flowery as a florist's window. When he raised his head, his gaze captured hers. She smiled a warm smile that melted his heart.

"Hasta la vista," she said, waving and sending him a grin.

"Hasta la vista," he murmured. He watched her walk across the patio, listening to the wind chimes give a faint *ting*. He glanced nearby and saw the colorful butterfly flutter with the breeze. He drew in a deep breath, thinking that right now seemed heaven on earth.

Joy's whining voice caught his attention. "Daddy."

"Sorry," he said again and lowered his head to study his tiles.

To his relief the game finally ended, even if too many minutes later. He sent the girls off to find some puzzles, then leaned back in the chair, his gaze drifting toward Felisa's doorway. Though she had access through the house, he noticed she rarely used that door—only when it was raining— and she always entered the main part of the house from the portico. He wondered why.

He closed his eyes, listening to the soft chiming sounds and the rustle of a twig or leaf skittering across the patio. When he heard Felisa's door close, he lifted his eyelid a millimeter and saw her heading his way. She'd changed her clothes to capri pants and a coral knit top that made him think of a sunset.

"Where's Nate?" he asked, straightening in the chair.

"Sleeping." She sat in the chair Faith had abandoned. "The game's over?"

"Thankfully." He grinned. "You spend every day doing this, and I'm moaning over an hour of dominos."

"You have better things to do with your time. I don't. That's my job."

"But you love it, Felisa. I see it on your face. You were meant to be a mother."

She tilted her head, a tender look filling her face. "However God can use me. That's what I do."

"And you do it so well."

"Thank you." She settled deeper into the chair and leaned her head back for a moment. "I visited with Maria today." Her voice sounded bittersweet. "I'd planned to take her to lunch, but I—I decided against it." She opened her eyes and shifted upward. "It's unbelievable how a few weeks can make such a difference."

"Difference? How?"

"She was happy to see me, but when I told her I was a nanny I saw her change. I'm sorry I said anything."

"She was envious?"

She gave a slight shrug. "I don't know if it was that. She seemed to just back away as if she couldn't handle my news." She ran her hand down her hair, then twirled a ringlet with her finger. "Working the fields is a hard life. Being a nanny probably sounds like a picnic."

He studied her face, not knowing how to respond. He could imagine what Maria had said when Felisa told her who she was working for.

"I told her I'd be back soon, but I think she didn't believe me."

"You tried to be her friend, Felisa. She'll probably think it over and wish she'd been friendlier."

"I understand. I might have felt the same way if I had been in her place."

"You're a compassionate woman. You always put the best light on everything."

She shook her head. "No. I really don't. I—" She faltered and didn't finish.

He longed to pursue the topic but sensed she'd backed away from him for a reason. Felisa had probably been thinking of Mrs. Drake. He wouldn't blame her for having negative feelings about the woman. "Did you enjoy church today?"

"Very much." Her expression went from a frown to a fleeting smile and stopped with another scowl. "Can I ask you a question?"

He leaned forward. "Sure."

"You'll probably think I'm silly."

"I'd never think you were silly."

"You might," she said, "when you hear this question. Is your God and the one I've worshipped all my life the same God?"

He drew his head back, startled by her words.

"See," she said.

"You surprised me, that's all." He pondered her query.

"It may sound like a strange question, but in my church in Mexico we revere the Lord. He commands us to follow His will and punishes us when we sin. We pray on our knees for forgiveness. I've seen people walk to the church on their knees to beg the Lord to—"

"Felisa."

She looked at him wide eyed. "Did I say something wrong?"

"No," he said, now understanding her worries. "We believe in the same God. It's not God who is different. It's tradition. God allows us to express our praise and thanksgiving in different ways. In your church, you come to God in reverence and quiet. We come to the Lord with joy because we know He has already forgiven our sins by giving us Jesus, who died on the cross for us." He looked at her quizzical expression. "You believe in Jesus."

"Yes."

"And the Holy Spirit."

"I do. It's just different. I like your church. I leave feeling happy rather than ashamed I am such a sinner."

"We're all sinners. Every one of us. But our sins are wiped clean by Jesus' blood shed for us. So we can rejoice. We can clap our hands and—"

"Raise them to heaven," she said, extending her hands upward in praise.

"That's right." He chuckled at her huge smile.

"I like that feeling. I think God wants us to smile when we thank Him."

"Have you read the Bible?"

"Bible?" Her eyes shifted as if in thought. "I've heard scripture read in church. The padre explained it to us."

He held up his finger. "Wait one minute." Chad darted into the house and found a study Bible, then hurried back. "Here. Read the Bible for yourself. Sometimes it's confusing, but most of it is clear. And if you have questions, we can talk about it."

She took the scriptures in her hand and ran her fingers over the cover. "My mother had a Bible. She kept records of births and deaths of the family. The Bible was like our family history."

He nodded. "Bibles have been used always to record family trees, but they're also meant to be read."

"Thank you. I'd like to read it."

"Start with the New Testament. It will be easier, and you'll read the story of Jesus, and then you'll understand why we are so joyful in church."

She placed the book against her chest and hugged it. "Good. I want to understand."

He wanted her to understand, too. Having her know the Lord meant everything to him. His heart yearned to love her as a wife, but he wanted her to love Jesus more than she loved him.

Felisa had touched him like no other woman had since Janie. He wanted to know Felisa's dreams and longings, her plans for the future, and, most of all, whether she had feelings for him. Sometimes he caught her watching him, her face filled with such tenderness it wrenched his heart. Other times she looked at him with wary eyes. He knew they were worlds apart in society's eyes, but in his she'd become the air he breathed, offering him a sense of wholeness.

ten

The summer sun hung low on the horizon, and the day's heat had permeated the house even with air-conditioning. Felisa stood in the doorway watching the girls finish their bath—their light brown hair now dark from shampooing and their soft cheeks rosy with the warm water.

"Ready?" she asked, knowing they wouldn't be, but it was time for bed.

"It's still daytime," Faith said, her usual whine making Felisa grin.

"I know," she said, encouraging Faith to smile back at her, "but it's always daylight when you go to bed. It'll be dark soon. It's eight thirty."

Faith raised her shoulders in a deep breath. "Okay." She dragged the okay out longer than a yardstick.

Nate's whimper came through the intercom, and Felisa paused, wanting to run to her son but knowing she didn't want to leave the four-year-old girls alone in the tub. As she listened, the cry faded, and she turned her attention back to the girls. Joy hadn't complained tonight, and she looked a little pale. That concerned Felisa. She grabbed two towels, and as the girls stood, she wrapped a towel around each. They stepped from the tub with her help, and she toweled them down, then handed each one her pajamas.

"You don't feel well, Joy?"

She gave a little shrug.

Felisa guided them into the bedroom, tucked them in, then headed for the door.

"What about our bedtime story?" Faith asked.

"I'll be right back," she said, hurrying to the bathroom for the thermometer.

When she returned she slipped it under Joy's tongue and grasped their Bible storybook, then sat on the end of Joy's bed. She waited a minute, then read the thermometer. "You have a fever. Before you go to sleep I'll give you some medicine." She patted the child's flushed cheek and opened the book.

"Today the story is about Samuel and Eli. Have you heard that story?"

"I think so," Faith said, curling on her side and pressing her hands beneath her cheeks.

"What do you remember about Eli?"

"He was old," Joy said.

"That's right. Let's listen to the story." She began to read how God called Samuel. "And Samuel hurried to Eli saying, 'Here I am; you called me.' Every time Eli sent him back to bed until the older man realized it was God who'd called. So Eli said to Samuel, 'The next time you hear the voice calling you say, "Here I am, Lord. I am Your servant."' So Samuel did what God told him to do, and he heard God's message."

The story's truth struck her; she'd learned so much from the children's Bible stories. She finished the story, gave Joy the medication, and snapped off the light. As she headed through the house to the patio, anxious to check on Nate, her mind sifted through her thoughts. How many times had God spoken to her and she hadn't recognized His voice? She'd prayed for guidance, but she'd missed what the Lord was telling her and had no idea how to hear Him.

Felisa grabbed a soft drink from the refrigerator and stepped into the portico. The sun's colors had touched the mountaintops, and a splash of coral and lavender mingled with the heavenly blue in an amazing display. As she stepped from beneath the portico to the patio, she halted. Chad had pulled the umbrella chair close to the fountain and was holding Nate on his knees and patting his back. The picture touched her.

"Sorry," she said, striding his way. "I was giving the girls their bath. I heard him, but—"

"It's no problem," Chad said. "You know I love to hold Nate." He motioned to the table. "Bring another chair over and sit with me. It's a pretty sunset."

"As always," she said, so aware of the gorgeous evening skies. She did as he said and returned with the chair. "Joy has a fever."

He frowned. "Serious?"

"No, it's only a hundred. It's probably a summer cold. I gave her some medication. I'm sure she'll be fine in the morning."

"You care so much about the girls. It means a lot to me."

"They mean a lot to me," she said, wanting to add that he meant a great deal to her, too. She looked toward Nate. "Do you want me to do that?"

"Not on your life." He gave her a tender smile.

She stretched her legs in front of her and tilted her head back, breathing in a fresh breeze from the mountains as they cooled in the setting sun. Out of the corner of her eye, she watched Chad making gentle circles on Nate's back. The baby looked contented.

"I fed him a short time ago, so he shouldn't be hungry," she said.

"He wants attention. We all need that sometimes."

His words sounded melancholy, and her pulse tripped. Everyone needed to be loved and caressed. She'd been without that kind of relationship since she'd married Miguel. His love had become rough and his drunken words, vile.

Silence settled over them until Chad turned toward her. "Do you understand what I'm saying?"

She nodded. "The world's a lonely place when we don't have someone special to share it with."

His gaze captured hers. "I've found someone, Felisa."

Her stomach twisted, and she felt startled by her dismay and confusion. When had he found the time to meet someone? "You mean. . ." She couldn't find the words.

"I mean I've found someone who makes me want to live again, who's opened my eyes to what I've been missing."

Her hand trembled, and she couldn't look at him. "I'm so happy for you, Cha—" She had started to call him Chad, but the familiarity didn't seem right now.

Chad shifted his hand and rested it against hers, which had been clutching the chair arm. "I don't think you understand me."

"I do," she said. "You've found a lady friend who—"

He held up his hand to stop her, his eyes so amazingly tender, she thought she might melt.

"I've found you, Felisa."

Her lungs felt as if they had collapsed. She fought for air, gasped, then breathed again. "Me?" She forced herself to look at him, to see if he were laughing or teasing or—

"This is no joke. I know what others might think, and I've fought the attraction myself until I'm sick with trying. I can't fight my feelings any longer. I won't."

Dazed, she could only shake her head. He'd spoken aloud the dream she'd been ashamed to admit. She loved his girls, and he gave her delight with his smile and warmth. Yet she knew it was impossible. He'd just said the same. Others would scorn their friendship, let alone feelings stronger than that.

"Do you have feelings for me, Felisa? Any at all?"

His question dropped into her head and unsettled her. "I—I—"

"Please." He lifted her hand from the chair arm and held it in his. "I sensed that you—"

His voice sounded as if it failed him, and Felisa could not find the words to answer. What would God have her say? Should she answer with her heart or her reason?

"May He give you the desire of your heart." The scripture verse came out of nowhere and filled her mind. Wishful thinking? She faltered mid-thought. Samuel had heard God's voice and didn't recognize it. Had this verse come from the Lord?

Felisa lifted her gaze to Chad's. His jaw ticked with tension, and she raised her hand and pressed her palm against his cheek. "You're asking the impossible."

"That's not what I asked you. Do you have any feelings for me? That's what I want to know."

She pulled away her gaze and sensed his jaw tightening. "Yes," she whispered.

His free hand touched her cheek; his tender caress rippled down her back and warmed her heart. "Thank you. I know it's soon, and it's not easy."

"I love the girls, Chad. I think you are a wonderful father and a gentle man. I admire you from the depths of my heart. I've dreamed of this moment, but I fear it will only open us to so much hurt."

"Not if God is on our side, Felisa. I've prayed that the Lord would guide my words and actions. I would never do anything to purposely hurt you."

"I know that. I would never think that—" She stumbled over the phrase, remembering her earlier suspicion. She lowered her hand from his face. "One time I did question your motives for helping me. I was frightened, but I know better now."

"My motives?" His eyes looked concerned, and he lowered his hand and grasped hers.

"I didn't know what you wanted of me, and then I feared you wanted to take Nate from me."

His face grew ashen. "I would never have done that. I would never have thought to do that."

"I realize that now, now that I know you, but before, I looked for motives." She felt starved for oxygen. She gulped for air, then forced herself to calm down. "I'd never been treated so well. Never. You can understand why I would wonder about your reasons for being so kind."

"I do understand," he said, a frown settling on his face.

But Felisa studied his expression. "You probably don't. You haven't lived a life like mine, not that you haven't had your own sorrows, but life isn't easy for migrant workers. We're resented and distrusted by many people. Our lives are difficult and insecure, but it's usually the best we can do."

"You're right. I doubt if I can even imagine how it is."

The sun had settled behind the mountains, and a hazy glow tipped the distant peaks. Shadows lowered around them and took the edge from the day. The world seemed more peaceful and private. Felisa wondered in this quiet moment if she could ask the question that had haunted her for so long.

"I know you're a kind man. You're good to your workers. You've been more than kind to me, and I know you love Nate, and I just wondered—"

She saw him turn toward her, a heavy burden in his eyes.

A prayer rose inside her, a prayer for God's help to find the right words. "From the beginning, you've been attached to Nate." The words blurted from her. "You've been. . .interested in him, and that's not like most men. I want to know why."

Chad's shoulders slumped as if he'd been run down by a tractor in a lettuce field. His eyes darkened, and he raised his hand and rubbed the nape of his neck. She heard him sigh as he shook his head. "I had a son. He died."

Felisa's chest knotted, then coiled its way to her throat. "Died?" She felt breathless. "I didn't know you had a son."

"How would you?" He looked into the dusky sky for a moment, his hands unmoving in his lap. "It's difficult to talk about." His eyes glazed, and he looked beyond her as if remembering. "That was the saddest day of my life."

Felisa struggled to find her voice. "Chad, I'm so sorry. So horribly sorry." She swallowed back her tears. "What happened?"

"The umbilical cord became compressed during delivery, and before they could take him, he was gone."

Felisa lost the battle. Tears sprang into her eyes as she imagined the grief Chad and his wife had felt. "How horrible for you and your wife. I can't imagine bearing that kind of pain." She wondered if his wife gave up living from a broken heart. He'd never said why she died.

His head drooped, and he didn't speak for a moment. "Horrible for *me*," he said finally.

"For you?"

His gaze captured hers. "My wife died that day before she knew about our son."

❧

My wife died that day. Chad hadn't heard those words spoken in nearly two years. The double grief seemed more than he could bear, not only for himself but also for his two little toddlers who needed a mother's love. If not for the Lord, Chad would have given up on life. But his faith had sustained him, probably the same as Felisa's faith had sustained her.

He lifted his gaze and, in the shadowed light, saw tears in Felisa's eyes.

He grasped her hand and cupped his fingers around it. "I've learned to accept it. I know there's a purpose for everything under heaven, but the memory is still raw. Sad days like that one seem to live in the memory without fading."

She nodded and brushed the tears from her eyes. "Miguel

didn't know about Nate."

"But he would have been overjoyed."

Her gaze darkened. "I wasn't sure how he'd take it."

Chad's tension heightened, and he questioned, "How he'd take it?" He couldn't imagine a man not overjoyed to be a father.

"We depended on both our wages. A baby would only complicate matters in his eyes."

"But you wanted Nate." He saw a flicker of anxiety in her face.

"If I'm honest, no. I didn't want to bring a child into the ugly world I lived in. Moving from place to place is hard enough for adults. For kids, it's horrible. It's bad for their education and for them to feel safe, especially—"

Chad tried to control the frown that slipped to his face. "But I—"

"You look surprised. Upset." Her face filled with sadness. "When I learned I was expecting a baby, the amazing thought of giving birth to another human being, the gift that God had given me, made me think differently. I looked forward to the day when I would feel life, a tiny speck growing inside me. Despite my worries, having a baby seemed astounding to me."

"I can't imagine not being excited. Having a child is such a blessing. I have a successful business and a nice home, but Joy and Faith, in spite of their bad days, make my life seem purposeful."

"They're beautiful girls, and expecting the third must have given you and your wife happiness. I would have felt the same in your shoes, but you weren't married to someone like Miguel. You would see the situation differently."

"You said you weren't happy."

She lowered her head and seemed to stare at her woven fingers tensed in her lap. "He was a drunk. Every night he left for the bar and spent the little money we had. I hid my pay so we had food and sometimes a place to sleep, but he often forced me to give it to him. He would—"

"Forced you?" Chad's hands had knotted to fists. "What do you mean? Did he hurt you?"

"Sometimes when he was drunk." She shook her head as if the motion would chase away the memories. "I don't want to talk about it."

Chad rose and drew her into his arms. He felt her slender body, trembling against his, her head pressed against his shoulder. He could smell the scent of sandalwood and citrus wrapping around them. His chest tightened, wanting to protect her from hurt, wanting to cushion her against rumors, wanting to warm her with his love and respect. Yet he couldn't until she understood the depth of his feelings, until she trusted him.

She drew back and looked into his eyes. "I've never told anyone about Miguel. No one."

He caressed her. "Then it's time you did. It eats you up inside if you don't."

"And it's caused me not to trust. Miguel said he loved me, but he didn't."

"He did," Chad said, "but the drink became his greatest lover instead of you. He was ashamed and abused you because it was his love for you that caused him to feel guilt. Alcohol can turn good people into monsters."

"I know," she whispered into his chest.

He tilted her chin upward. "Let's go somewhere tomorrow night. Just the two of us. I'll see if Juanita can stay on. She sits for me when I have evening meetings."

Seconds ticked past before she answered. "Are you sure?"

"I'm positive. Let's drive into Monterey or Carmel for dinner, some nice place where—"

"Chad." Her voice was as soft as the flutter of a butterfly's wings.

His heart gave a tug. "What is it?" He gazed into her concerned face.

"We can't go anyplace too nice. I don't have the right clothing for—"

"I'll tell you what. Let's pick up a quiet dinner somewhere, and then we'll go shopping for a few things. I owe you a bonus for taking care of the girls so much while Mrs. Drake was still here. That wasn't your job, but you did it anyway. What do you say?"

"You don't owe me for that. I love spending time with the girls. I watched them change from two mean-spirited children to two little girls who love to play."

He brushed his hand down her thick, dark hair. "You let me decide about that. I can ask Juanita or even Gloria to watch the children, and we'll go to the Barnyard. You'll find some nice things there."

"The barnyard? But—"

Her face flickered with confusion. He wanted to laugh, but he held back. He could only imagine what she'd pictured in her mind. "It's a good place to shop. Trust me on this."

She gave a slight nod, and he could only grin, thinking of tomorrow.

eleven

All day Monday Felisa's nerves seem frayed. A date with Chad seemed far beyond any reality she could have imagined. She'd dreamed of it, but never in a million years had she thought it might come true. She'd relaxed about leaving the twins with Gloria when Joy had awakened feeling better, not perfect, but with a normal temperature.

She struggled between exhilaration and edginess. He'd offered to take her shopping, and she felt it inappropriate for him to buy her clothes. Since coming to live in the Garrison household, she'd been able to save a little money for the future, and tonight, if Chad seemed determined for her to buy herself something, she would insist on paying for the items.

Standing in front of her closet, Felisa surveyed what she owned—denim jeans, a couple of pairs of pants, a few blouses and knit tops, three skirts, two of which she'd worn to church—nothing fancy enough for a dinner at a nice restaurant. She didn't fit in that world anyway. Who was she kidding? The thought gripped her stomach and sent her heart on an elevator ride. She sank to the edge of the bed and lowered her face into her hands. What was she doing?

Lord, I'm so afraid I'm making a mistake. I'm frightened I'll be hurt, that my heart will be hurt. I'm putting this job in jeopardy, and that means going back to the fields. Why is this happening? Why?

Tears blurred her eyes as she looked toward her closet, amazed she'd accepted Chad's dinner offer. She'd allowed her heart to step on her reason. She couldn't afford to make a mistake. If she managed to get through tonight, that would be the end of her going out to dinner with her employer. What would people think? What did Juanita think? Felisa had been pleased the new housekeeper had agreed to babysit. But she longed to talk with Juanita, with someone who understood her position, who understood the problems she could face.

Felisa brushed the tears from her eyes. She forced herself from the mattress edge, strode back to the closet, and pulled out the skirt with brightly colored flowers on a blue background. She'd never worn it since she'd arrived at Chad's. Felisa studied her tops. She had a blue knit top nearly the same color. She held them together in the mirror. Not bad.

Felisa tossed the skirt and top onto the bed and opened her dresser drawer, searching for a wide woven leather belt that she hoped would match her sandals. She found it and tossed it onto the bed beside the skirt. She had a pendant—not gold—but it looked gold and the same metal hoop earrings. Maybe she could survive tonight.

She dressed with haste and headed down the inside hallway to the main part of the house. She could hear the girls in the spacious family room, and when she entered, Juanita looked up from changing Nate's diaper and gave her a tense smile. Felisa suspected Juanita had reservations about the date.

"I want to kiss Nate good night," Felisa said, crossing the room to Juanita. "Thank you for changing his diaper before you go home. You're making the job easier for Gloria." She hoped to see Juanita smile, but she didn't.

"You're welcome. I hope you have a nice evening." She stood to leave.

When Felisa entered the family room, Gloria grinned, and the twins abandoned their puzzles to greet her. She'd noticed both girls eyeing her skirt when she came through the doorway.

"That's pretty," Joy said, touching the fabric.

"You look nice," Faith added, giving her a questioning look.

Joy leaned against her, her lips nearly forming a pout.

Concern popped into Felicia's thoughts. "Do you feel sick again?"

She shook her head. "No, but why can't we go with you?"

"It'll be late when we get home," Felisa said, grasping for the first logical answer she could think of.

"Can we go next time?" Faith asked.

Felisa knelt beside them and wrapped her arms around their waists. "It's up to your daddy, but next time we can check with him. Okay?"

They nodded but lingered beside her while Gloria tried to draw them back to the puzzles.

Felisa heard Chad's brisk footsteps coming down the hall and watched both girls run to him with their arms open for a hug when he came into the room.

"Felisa said we could come with you next time," Faith said.

"That's not quite right," Felisa said, correcting them. "I said it's up to your daddy."

"Listen, sugar cakes," he said, bunching them both in his arms. "I promise. The next outing, you can come, too." He shifted his attention to Felisa and gave her an admiring look. "Ready?"

She nodded, fiddling with the shoulder strap of her bag to hide her nervousness.

He stretched his arm toward her. "We won't be too late, Gloria. Thanks for sitting with the girls and Nate."

"You're welcome, Mr. Garrison. Anytime."

He gave Gloria the wonderful smile that made Felisa melt when he smiled at her, then grasped Felisa's arm as he steered her toward the door.

"You look lovely," he said, once they were outside. "I've

never seen that outfit."

"I hope it's not too colorful."

"Not at all. You look beautiful, Felisa."

Her pulse raced as he opened the passenger door, and she settled inside. She placed her handbag on her lap and folded her hands, afraid to move or talk for fear she'd wake up. Then reality set in, and she wanted to wake up, afraid of what might happen to ruin her relationship with Chad.

Her mind tangling with unstable emotions, Felisa struggled to make even meaningless conversation. She looked out the passenger window, listening to the soft music that drifted from the radio. "Tell me about the barnyard. Is it something like a flea market?"

He glanced her way, a grin growing on his face, then burst into laughter. "You mean *the* Barnyard."

The barnyard. Isn't that what she'd said? She eyed him, wondering what he thought she'd said. "You told me we could go shopping at a barnyard, and I—"

He released the steering wheel with one hand and gave her arm a caress. "The Barnyard is a village of fine shops, galleries, and restaurants. It's made up of buildings called stables. Besides wonderful clothing, they have the gardens. It's really nice this time of year with so many flowers in bloom."

She could hardly speak because of her embarrassment. She'd pictured a real barnyard, not a shopping area—fine shops, he'd said—with flower gardens, art galleries, and places to eat. She didn't fit into a mall like that.

Silence settled over them, and she watched the scenery change as they took the Monterey Highway past the airport to Highway 1. Chad turned south, and Felisa remembered traveling this way to go to Carmel.

"You're quiet," he said, turning to look at her. "Are you okay?"

"I'm fine." She couldn't look at him.

"Are you upset because I laughed about the Barnyard? It's an easy mistake. It does sound like a flea market."

She heard an apologetic tone in his voice, and Felisa wished she hadn't let the situation upset her. "I'm naive about a lot of things. Fancy malls aren't the places I shop."

"I know that. Please forgive me for laughing."

She finally looked at him. His strong jawline tensed with his distress. "You're forgiven, but it's my problem. I feel silly that I made the mistake."

"You shouldn't. Let's forget it and have a good time."

She glanced at her flowered skirt, realizing she probably looked too casual or gaudy for the other shoppers. "Am I dressed okay? I don't want to embarrass you."

He released a sigh. "How could you embarrass me? You look gorgeous. You're a beautiful woman, Felisa, and if people look at you, it's not because you don't look appropriate. It's because they are envious."

She didn't believe a word of it, but his comment made her feel better. She brushed her hand over the cotton skirt. She liked cotton. She didn't need fancy clothes and furs. She wouldn't feel like herself in anything too fine.

They settled into an amiable silence while Felisa watched the landscape race by. When they passed Ocean Avenue, she knew they'd go around the downtown area of Carmel. She straightened in the seat, curious as to this barnyard place he'd told her about.

Chad made a turn away from the ocean, and soon he guided the sedan into a large parking area. "Here we are," he said, helping her from the car. "You can already see why I like this." He gestured toward the buildings ahead of her.

Felisa took in the rustic stable-style buildings with wide pine siding, stained in warm brownish hues, rising around her. As they followed the path, the stone walkway led them past lush gardens of poppies, snapdragons, cosmos, shasta daisies, lilies, and roses that trailed along the rocky slopes from the three levels. Felisa admired the vibrant trumpet vine and bougainvillea. The beauty took her breath away. "It's unbelievable, Chad."

He glided his arm around her back and gave her a squeeze. "So are you."

She sent him a grin, unable to respond with words. His fresh woodsy scent wrapped around her, and though his comment had addled her, she felt more secure and admired than she had in many years.

"Let's walk through the area so you can see it," he said, "and then we'll have dinner. Sound okay?"

"Sounds wonderful," Felisa said, unable to take her eyes from the unique setting.

Chad kept his arm around her as they wandered through the winding paths, gazing at shops that displayed breathtaking apparel, bath soaps and lotions, and gorgeous artwork. She wanted to press her nose against the windows and drink in the wonder. Chad guided her past a gurgling manmade brook, then through an open-air patio with an outdoor fireplace. She didn't know which way to look.

When she noticed him eyeing her, she grinned. "I don't know what to say. I've never seen anything like this before."

"It's time you did," he said, letting his arm drop from her shoulders so he could grasp her hand. "Hungry?"

She felt a hollow in her stomach and admitted she was.

"Then let's go back down to the first level. We'll eat there and shop later."

Felisa agreed, but the idea of shopping here disturbed her. She didn't have enough money to pay for the clothing in these wonderful shops. She could only imagine the price tags that hung on the lovely blouses and skirts, the dresses and shoes she saw in the store windows.

As they returned to the lower level, she walked with her hand in Chad's, his strong fingers engulfing her smaller hand. Feeling overwhelmed, she clung to him.

He steered her toward the Big Sur Barn, then to Bahama Billy's. She gazed at the small panes of the white-trimmed windows, looking like pictures she'd seen in magazines, and trellises covered with red vining bougainvillea. Stepping inside, Felisa felt as if she'd sailed away to another country. A buffet near the entrance was studded with Jamaican art pieces including the bust of a man with tight braids covered by a colorful cap. The pale green walls and ceiling were decorated with murals of palm fronds, and palm trees stood at intervals in large pots, bringing the outdoors inside.

The hostess led them to a table, and above her on the wall, Felisa eyed a colorful piece of art. She chuckled when she noticed many of the paintings were in wavy frames that looked as if she were viewing them through a rippling stream. The rounded-back chairs had cushioned seats in a muted print beside red-topped tables with real flowers and dark green china. She clenched her jaw, afraid she was gaping.

The waitress waited until they were seated, then handed them each a menu. When she'd taken their drink orders, she walked away to give them time to study the menu.

Felisa opened the colorful folder and scanned the many Jamaican-style choices: jerk chicken, mango crab bisque, coconut prawns, Kahlúa pork, barbequed ribs, and steaks. But her focus kept slipping to the price of each meal, and the cost unsettled her.

Chad sat across from her, looking over the choices.

When she felt his gaze on her, she shrugged. "I can't decide. Everything sounds so good."

"Most everything is. Wait until you taste their calypso cornbread. It's *ciabatta* bread sliced and served with hot corn kernels, garlic butter, and cheese with Serrano chilies. Nothing else like it."

Her mind spun with the choices and the cost. She could never afford to eat in a nice restaurant. Never.

ॐ

Chad gazed at Felisa's serious face as she perused the menu. He guessed this was a special treat for her. Today was an amazing event for him, too. "You're having a good time?"

She lifted her gaze slowly, a sweet smile curving her lovely lips to reveal even white teeth. One of her well-formed brows tilted in a beguiling arch. "I don't know which way to look. Everything is so wonderful. I suppose it's boring to you."

He rested his fingers over hers and pressed her small hand in his, amazed at the mixture of emotions that coiled through him—joy, surprise, tenderness. He leaned closer to her ear. "I've been here many times, but this is the first time I've seen the place through new eyes, and I'm enjoying it so much more."

She tilted her head and gazed at him with her dark brown eyes. "What do you see that I don't?"

"I see you."

She shook her head, her thick hair bouncing against her shoulders. "You're being silly."

"I'm being truthful." The delight of having her beside him bounded in his chest. "You make me forget my cares. You make me happy."

She squeezed his hand. "Happiness is within yourself. I can't give it to you."

Her wisdom astounded him, but he knew she'd learned that from her difficult life. "You help me find it, Felisa. You've given me the map."

He lifted her hand to his lips and pressed her soft skin.

Felisa's gaze followed his movement, and he feared he'd upset her; but when he looked he saw her cheeks had flushed a lovely pink.

As he lowered his hand, the waitress returned with their iced tea and lemon and was ready to take their order. "What would you like, Felisa?"

She gazed at the menu, and then at him. "It's all so—"

He held up his hand to stop her. It was expensive, but she was worth every penny. "Order whatever you'd like."

Finally she looked at the waitress. "Is the meat loaf good?"

Chad shook his head. She'd chosen the least expensive dinner on the menu.

"It's our specialty," the waitress said. "The loaf is wrapped in bacon and served smoky and crusty. It's everyone's favorite, and it comes with mashed potatoes and broccolini."

"I'll take that," she said.

"Give her a Bahama Billy salad with that. Make that two. One for me."

The woman jotted down the order. He added the blackened mahimahi with wasabi potatoes and their calypso cornbread.

He sipped his drink, watching Felisa's gaze dart from one table to the next. She watched patrons enter, and when she dropped her focus to her print skirt and plain top, he suspected she was worried about her appearance. "You look lovely, Felisa."

She flushed again, as if embarrassed she'd been caught in the act. "I can't afford items like these women. I have no use for such nice clothes anyway."

But she did, and he would tell her later. "We'll visit some shops after dinner. Donlé has everyday wear, and Mary's Boutique has nice dresses."

"But I can't—"

"You deserve a bonus. Please give me the pleasure of buying a couple of things for you."

She sank back in her chair, studying him as if looking for his motive again. He'd already told her how much he cared for her, but she obviously couldn't comprehend the depth of his feelings. Neither could he.

He let the conversation drift to the children and their preschool classes in the fall, the floral pathways they'd just wandered, the weather, and Gloria's love of the girls. Felisa was pleased with that, but something seemed to trouble her when he mentioned Juanita. He wanted to probe, but he decided to let it drop, hoping it was nothing serious. He also avoided the topic of shopping or of his feelings. This wasn't the place to delve into those issues that brought him great pleasure yet deep concern.

The food arrived, and the conversation turned to comments about the meal. They sank into their own silence; yet his gaze continued to settle on Felisa's lovely face, the delight he saw in her eyes and her haunting smile.

After they'd lingered over coffee and he'd paid the bill, he glanced at his watch and realized they should begin shopping before the time ran out. He'd never been more content than to sit beside Felisa after dinner and talk about nothing of consequence.

As they stepped outside, Chad felt a hand on his shoulder, and he spun around, surprised to see a familiar face. "Brook. How've you been?"

"Great, and you look well," he said, eyeing Felisa. "Very well, in fact."

Chad didn't like his ogling. "Felisa, this is Brook Garner. He owns a farm near Monterey. We sit on an agricultural committee together."

"Hello," she said, backing away as if uncomfortable.

Chad longed to put a protective arm around her, but with Brook's leer he stopped himself.

"Brook, this is Felisa Carrillo. She's the twins' nanny and—"

"Nanny." A taunting grin settled on his face. "My, my."

Chad saw Felisa shrink backward, moving away toward the path, and he felt helpless.

"You've got a good thing going with the sweet little nanny," Brook said. "You can send her to my house anytime."

Chad grasped his arm. "She deserves more respect than that, Brook."

"She's Mexican, Chad. What do you expect me to think?"

"Think this." He stood up to the man, nose to nose. "Hispanic, American, African-American, Chinese—I don't care. Everyone deserves respect unless you have the facts to know otherwise. If I hear one snide comment about her, I'll—"

"Chad, I was pulling your leg." Brook took a step backward. "You can date who you want to, but you can't expect everyone to have the same view you do." He gave a head toss toward Felisa. "Those people work in my fields."

"And they work in mine, where they receive a decent wage and respect. You should do the same." Chad shook his head. "You claim to be a Christian man. I've heard you. Tonight you'd better sit down with the Good Book and read 1 Corinthians 4. Then talk to me."

He gave Brook's arm an amiable shake. "Sorry about this, but I can't stand back and allow you to insult someone I care about very much." He took a step toward Felisa. "I'll see you at the dinner party next week." He said good-bye and turned.

"Chad."

He heard a woman call and pivoted to see Brook's wife, carrying a designer shopping bag and waving to him.

"Hello, Colleen," he said, waving back. "I'll see you soon."

He clasped Felisa's arm and headed down the brick walkway toward Mary's Boutique.

ൠ

Felisa sat in her room with her new garments spread on the bed. She'd entered the stores with Chad, afraid to look at the price tags and feeling out of place there. She didn't think Chad understood.

She'd wanted to turn and run; but he tucked his arm around her waist or held her hand, and the sensation covered the scattered moments of discouragement she felt. She feared the saleswomen were judging her—maybe because of the clothes she wore or maybe from prejudice. Could it be her own feelings of being out of place? Unworthy?

Chad had guided her through the shops, showing her racks with skirts and lacy tops. She'd tried to read the tags, but he'd sometimes nudge her hand away, letting her know price didn't matter. Finally he'd encouraged her to buy a teal blue pantsuit with a scoop-neck knit top in a lighter blue print. She loved the three pieces, and they felt so smooth on her. When she stepped from the dressing rooms to the large mirror, his smile had lifted her spirit.

At another store he'd shown her a party dress in deep coral. She tried it on and admired the rich fabric that clung to her form then swirled to her calves. She'd never seen anything more lovely. Chad had risen to meet her when she'd stepped from behind the dressing room's louvered doors and told her she looked like royalty. She'd never been told anything like that before.

On the way to the car, he led her to a shoe store and insisted she buy a pair of dressy tan sandal pumps and a matching clutch bag to carry with the coral dress. The gifts had cost more than any bonus she deserved, but he insisted it gave him pleasure, and seeing the light in his eyes, she knew he meant it.

Pushing the memory aside, Felisa hung the garments in her closet, fingering the soft fabric and admiring the lovely lines. She placed the shoes and handbag on the closet shelf, wondering where she would ever wear anything that stylish.

Turning from the closet, Felisa grabbed one of the shopping bags and began shoving the wrappings into it. While she worked, her mind slipped back to the man Chad had met coming out of the restaurant—Brook, if she remembered correctly. She'd been uncomfortable when she noticed he and Chad were having words. She'd never seen Chad so upset, and she knew it was her presence that had caused the spark of anger. Chad had said nothing about it to her, which was his way, and she hadn't wanted to ruin the evening by asking. After depositing the tags and tissue into the single shopping bag, she set it by her wastebasket. She'd take it to the trash later.

Felisa sank to the edge of her bed and rubbed her temples. Her rampant thoughts hammered in her head, and she tossed herself back against the pillow, wondering what God had in store for her. The sermons at the new church had given her hope and deepened her trust. She knew the Lord was her strength and shield, her rock and hiding place, but when she tried to put it into practice, she failed.

Nate gave a cry, and Felisa pulled herself up to a sitting position, then rose and strode to the crib. She lifted him in her arms and rocked him as she headed toward the bed. Nate had grown so much since his birth. At nearly two months old he'd become a little person, his bright eyes gazing at her and his tiny hands clasping her finger. He seemed to know her voice, and he kicked his feet when he heard the twins. They were so tender with him that it made her nearly weep with happiness.

She recalled her arrival at this wonderful home. She'd been frightened and confused, fearing the worst, but Chad had proven his word, and she'd touched his life by helping his two little bookend girls to be more lovable. All they needed was affection, attention, and assurance. She'd given those things to them, and so had Chad. He'd learned from her example and now spent more time with the twins. He doted on them to be exact, and they loved every minute of his time with them.

Felisa grinned, knowing the girls weren't perfect. They still had their bad moments—Faith's whining and stomping, Joy's quiet anger and narrowed eyes sending her a laser of contempt—but most of the time they were sweet and innocent.

Nate wiggled his arms, and she felt his diaper. He needed a change, and she drew him closer, kissing his cheek and cuddling him against her. She'd grown to love Chad's way with him. He loved her son, too, and the memory filled her with sadness when she thought of the day Chad had revealed that he'd lost his wife and son.

Since her faith had strengthened, Felisa had learned that when Christians left this world they walked into the arms of Jesus. But when Chad's wife and son had gone to heaven, it had left his arms horribly empty and with such a burden to bear.

Life. She felt so ignorant, so lacking when she thought of God's infinite ways. How could she, a mere mortal, ever understand God's plan? Chad's pastor had explained that people might not understand now but would when they met God face-to-face. She would have to wait for that day.

twelve

With the girls occupied with a cartoon movie on the television, Felicia wandered toward the kitchen, her heart in her throat. As she neared the room, she could hear Juanita working, her knife smacking against the wood cutting board.

"Hola," she said, resting her elbows on the kitchen counter. "What are you making?"

"Apple pie."

She studied the woman who'd become her friend. A new reserve seemed to barricade their normally friendly relationship, and Felisa feared she knew why. She waited until Juanita stopped wielding the knife and had dropped the sliced apples into a readied piecrust. After she'd sprinkled the sugar and cinnamon onto the apples, Juanita lowered the top crust, crimped the edges, and made hasty slits in the top. She carried the pie to the oven, opened the door, and slid it inside.

When she turned around she faced Felisa. "You want to talk?"

"Yes," she said, her voice coming out a whisper.

Juanita motioned to a kitchen chair, and Felisa accepted her offer by sitting. When Juanita joined her she carried two glasses of iced tea and handed one across the table to Felisa. "I'm all ears."

Though her words were sharp, Felisa heard concern in her voice. "You know what I want to talk about."

"I do."

"Then what can I say? I–I'm—" Moisture blurred Felisa's eyes as she looked at the one woman she'd counted on. She lowered her face in her hands and let the tears flow.

Juanita didn't move while Felisa let her worry and fears flood from her being. Then the older woman rose, and the warmth of her hand spread across Felisa's back while the tenderness comforted her.

"What were you thinking, Felisa?" Juanita asked.

She wiped her eyes with her fists, then raised her head. "I wasn't. A person can't think with her heart."

"I know," she said. With a gentle caress, she straightened her back and looked in Felisa's eyes. "I saw it coming and not just from one direction. What could I do to warn either of you?"

Felisa lowered her head and shook it. "Nothing." She knew that love happened. It was like a corralled wild horse with a mind of its own and a driving will to be freed.

"Mr. Garrison has been lonely since his wife died. He'd turned inward and even lost track of his little girls. They were a mess. You know that."

Felisa nodded.

"Then you came along, bringing a little son and a heart full of love. You lavished the girls with your affection, and you pried open their father's heart."

"But I didn't mean to. I knew it was an impossible situation. I'm Hispanic. Worse. I'm a migrant worker who—"

Juanita stopped her with her hand on hers. "You're a beautiful woman who fell into a bad lot. You didn't want the life you found yourself in."

"No, I didn't. I hated it, but I figured it was all I had. I managed." She knew her definition of *managed* was a bad one.

"You survived," Juanita said as if hearing her thoughts. "You deserve better. Everyone does." She backed away and settled in her chair.

Felicia drew in a deep breath for courage. "Then why are you angry at me? You're the one person I counted on to listen when I needed someone."

"I'm not angry. I'm concerned. I know you've had a hard life, and I know the one you're heading for will be difficult, as well. But—" She pushed the tumbler with her finger, leaving a trail of condensation on the table, her gaze distant as if she had more to say.

Felisa waited.

"But people can change." She lifted her gaze, and her lips moved into a faint smile. "You're a charming woman, as well as beautiful. They'll learn to love you, and they won't care where you came from. You're a bright woman. Very capable. Just don't let anyone hammer you down."

Felisa leaned her head back, releasing a ragged sigh. "I've kept this bottled inside me for so long, not believing where my heart was leading and so afraid of being hurt. Then Chad let me know how he felt. I distrusted him for so long. I feared he wanted Nate, that this was all a trick to take my son, and when that fear passed I still wanted to know his motivation."

"Motivation?" Juanita gave her a full grin. "God's Word. He lives it. I admire him."

"I realize that now. He bought me some new clothes. Did you know?"

Juanita shook her head.

"I wanted to pay him back, but I didn't have the money. He insisted he owed me for giving the girls so much attention while Mrs. Drake was still here. I know it was just an excuse, because he knows I don't have much."

"Don't question the reasons or his generosity. I'm shocked to hear myself say this, but love him, Felisa. He's a good man, and you're a good woman. I've watched you with the girls and Nate. You're a great mother and a hard worker, you appreciate kindness, and you believe in the Lord. That's a nice bunch of qualities to add to being lovely and charming."

She rose, walked to Felisa's side, and gave her a hug. "Be happy. Block your ears from the comments and close your eyes to the looks. They'll go away with time and prayer."

"Thank you," Felisa said, forcing the air around the lump in her throat. "Thanks so much."

❧

Chad opened the car door, and the girls scurried out, anxious to get inside. He'd promised them they could go on the next outing, and Felisa had mentioned the Monterey Bay Aquarium. She'd never been there, and he knew the girls were the perfect age to enjoy the hands-on adventures. Nate wasn't old enough to enjoy the day, but Chad hadn't wanted to leave him behind, so they'd brought him, stroller and all. He'd grown to love the boy as his own. The words filled his heart. He loved the child's mother, too, more than he could put into words.

"Hurry, Daddy!" Faith called, rushing toward the entrance.

"Hold on," he said, getting out his wallet to pay for the tickets.

The exuberant bunch bounded through the doors and bounced beside him at the ticket booth.

"If you hurry, you can see the shark feeding at the Kelp Forest," the woman said.

"Hurry, Daddy!" Faith yelled again, tugging at him.

"Hold on, Faith." He grinned at the woman. "Which way?"

"Just to the left," she said, motioning in that direction. "It starts at eleven thirty."

He paid for the tickets, and the girls scampered in front of him, veered left, then stopped to gape at the three-story-high tank. Chad grinned, noticing they were a little apprehensive when they saw the huge sea creatures—leopard sharks, sting-rays, black rockfish, and wolf-eels—gliding past the massive window and weaving through the fronds of kelp.

"Let's get closer," he said, encouraging the girls forward.

"They need their daddy to protect them," Felisa said.

"I guess." He gave her a wink and lifted Nate from the stroller, and they maneuvered their way into the group of people surrounding the three-story window.

In moments the stream of light from above the tank was broken by a diver, who plunged into the fray and was surrounded by large schools of fish. When he opened his bag of food, they swarmed around him. A huge shark headed for the diver, and Chad held his breath until the diver fed the fish and it soared away. He chuckled at himself. Obviously the diver would be safe, but watching the scene made him question his certainty.

Chad glided his arm around Felisa's back while the narrator explained the Kelp Forest, the kinds of fish in the tank, and what they ate. The girls were glued to the window, their eyes as wide as lettuce heads. Occasionally they looked toward them with broad smiles, then focused again on the tank. Nate cooed in his arms, and Chad felt Felisa nestle closer to him. He gazed down, admiring her well-defined lips that looked as soft as velvet. He longed to kiss her, but he hadn't done so yet. She needed time to trust his love and to accept what he hoped to offer her.

"Do you like this?" he asked, leaning close to her ear.

Her grin answered his question. "I feel like a little kid. I'm so excited."

"I love being here with you and the girls. Everything seems so much more purposeful now. I did things with the girls before, but I felt alone and it made me sad. Now it's different."

She only nodded, though he'd hoped she might have said more. He knew she loved being with him. He could see it in her demeanor, but he also knew she struggled with the situation. His mind slipped back to Brook Garner. The man's rudeness and disdain made Chad feel sick. Even before Felisa entered his life, he'd tried to be kind to those who worked his fields. He felt guilty when he knew some didn't have proper living conditions, but he did what he could to make life better for them.

Felisa's gaze had settled on him, and he turned to look at her, managing a smile.

"You're thinking," she said.

Her eyes searched his, showing her concern beneath her calm exterior. "Just some work issues," he said, hoping to cover his unpleasant memories. He tilted his head toward the girls. "Do you think we can pry them away from the tank?"

She chuckled. "I doubt it."

Before he moved forward to get their attention, the narration stopped, and people began to drift away. He returned Nate to the stroller, then called the twins and steered them across the skywalk to the Drifters' Galley and the Outer Bank. The journey took longer than he wanted, since they had to pass through the aquarium gift shop.

Chad clamped his hand on each girl's shoulder. "We'll stop back later. Okay? Let's go see the biggest fish tank in the whole world."

Joy's eyes widened. "Bigger than the one we just saw?"

He nodded, relieved he had her attention.

Faith looked dubious. "How big is it?"

"Do you know how much milk is in a gallon?"

"The big jugs?" Faith asked, holding her hands apart to demonstrate.

"That's it. Well, this tank holds more than a million gallons of water. A million is one with lots of zeros. This long." He demonstrated with his hands.

"I want to see it," she said, accepting his hand.

At the next display, bluefin tuna powered past the windows,

sea turtles meandered by, and massive hammerhead sharks circled inches away from the thick Plexiglas of the Kelp Forest.

"Look, Daddy," Joy said, pointing to a huge school of carrot-colored jellyfish drifting past. Next she spotted comb jellies that pulsed with colored bands of light as they glided by.

He let the girls watch for a while, one hand on the stroller and his other hand wrapped around Felisa's, his mind reeling with the sense of family he hadn't felt since Janie died. Finally he dragged them away to the second floor and located the touching pools. Even Felisa knelt beside the tanks to handle the rays and starfish of all sizes and colors.

Chad's heart raced, feeling happiness that had eluded him for so long. The same sense of family, of belonging together, washed over him. He knelt beside Felisa, drawing in her flowery scent, and rested his hand on her shoulder, his fingers playing with her tight curls. He longed to run his fingers through her hair and capture her lips beneath his.

He rose, afraid of the feelings that stirred in him. He needed to give her time. Yet he'd waited so long even to think about loving again, and now that he'd found the one, he didn't want to lose her.

❧

Outside, the salty breeze carried a faint hint of fish. Felisa couldn't help but smile at the girls and herself as they explored the sea life at the aquarium. She'd become one of the children, delving into the water to capture a ray and walking along the lines of water troughs dotted with colorful live starfish.

"That was fun, wasn't it?" she said to the girls as they bounced beside her, carrying stuffed animals from the gift shop. Faith had wanted a plush octopus, and Joy had chosen a toy jellyfish. Felisa loved the little creatures and had almost asked for one for herself. Nate was too young to use as an excuse. She feared the button eyes on the animals could be dangerous, but she'd purchased a knit shirt for him decorated with brightly colored fish.

"Let's walk down Cannery Row to the restaurant. We can have an early dinner." Chad pointed ahead to the red arch and row of old cannery buildings. "There's a Mexican restaurant there, or we could eat at Bubba Gumps."

"Bubba Gumps!" the girls called out.

"Run Forrest Run!" Joy sang out.

Chad looked at her, and she nodded. "Sounds good to me. I can get Mexican anytime." She chuckled at her little joke, and so did Chad.

Felisa pushed the stroller, and he tucked his arm around her waist as the girls skipped on ahead. Soon a large pink sign greeted them, emblazoned with BUBBA GUMPS. They left the sidewalk and headed through the parking lot to the weathered-looking grayish blue building with ornate embellishment at the top. Inside, Felisa didn't know which way to look. The movie *Forrest Gump* played on screens all over the restaurant, Forrest's bench sat near the door, and memorabilia adorned the nooks.

"We're between lunch and dinner, so the place isn't packed," Chad said. "Usually we have to wait."

The hostess greeted them, then led them to a table along a window that captured a panoramic view of Monterey Bay. The girls wanted to be closest to the window, so they shuffled around, allowing Chad to sit nearer Felisa. She liked the arrangement.

"What's that?" Felisa asked, pointing to a bucket with two signs that looked like license plates.

Chad chuckled. "If you want the waitress, you flip it to STOP FORREST STOP. If you don't need service, you put up the RUN FORREST RUN sign." He flipped the sign to STOP FORREST STOP, and in a moment, a waiter came to take their soft-drink order.

The novelty made Felisa smile, adding another bit of happiness to her day. She eyed the menu with so many choices. She'd learned to stop worrying about prices. Chad had given her a sweet lecture that she should order what she wanted. She spotted the baby back ribs, and her stomach growled. The girls wanted the Bucket of Trash, a pail filled with all kinds of seafood, probably enough for everyone.

"Let's just order a variety and share," Chad said.

"I love that idea," she said, wanting to try so many things.

When the waiter arrived with their drinks, they placed the order, and the girls asked if they could look out the other large window nearby.

"Don't be gone long," Chad said. "And don't go any farther than right there." He pointed to the open area where they wouldn't be in anyone's way and he could watch them.

The girls agreed and hurried off, leaving Felisa and Chad alone, except for Nate, for the first time that day.

"Thanks for the wonderful trip. You know I've never been to the aquarium. I've never been anyplace really, so this is as much fun for me as it is for the girls."

He scooted closer and wove his fingers through hers. "It's more fun for me, too. I love watching your face glow with excitement. You're so beautiful—inside and out."

"Thank you. The inside is most important to me. You know that."

"I do, and that's why I love you so much."

Love you so much. The words sailed across the space and floated into her thoughts. Did he really love her? She knew he cared. He'd told her she meant so much to him, but love? She managed to smile, afraid he'd think something was wrong.

Chad lifted her hand and kissed her fingers. His lips felt soft and warm, and her chest tightened at his gentle touch. Years ago, when Miguel came near her she cringed, fearing he would backhand her or worse. With Chad, his touch had always been a sweet caress, one that left her feeling safe and cherished.

He shifted to check on the twins, then turned back to her. "I've been wanting to talk with you about something, and I hope you'll say yes."

Her pulse tripped along her arms. "Talk about what?"

"Felisa, you look upset, and I haven't even asked you yet."

"I'm sorry. I'm afraid of hearing bad news."

His eyes filled with tenderness, and the look made her catch her breath.

"I'd like you to go with me to a dinner party." He held up his hand to keep her from responding. "You can think about it, but I'd like you to go with me."

"A dinner party? With your friends?"

"People from the agricultural society. Business people. It's a summer party they throw each year. Dinner, music, conversation."

She saw the urgency in his face, but the impossibility rose above her like a tidal wave. "Chad, I don't fit in with those people. You know how most of them feel about us, and I'm sure the word has spread about who I am. We work in their fields. They don't want to have us during a dinner party."

"Felisa, it's time you forget about the word *us* when you're talking about the fields. *Us* is you and me. That's the only *us* I want to hear. If people get to know you, they won't care anything about that. They'll find you as delightful as I do."

"But—" She grasped for reasons. She needed an excuse. No. No. She loved Chad, but this could never work. "Chad, I—"

"We have to do this sometime, Felisa. I'm not letting you

go that easily. You're precious to me. I care about you more than I can say." He flung his arms open in his fervor and nearly collided with a waitress passing by. He gave her a look of apology. "I want people to get to know you. I know it's not easy, but we can't stay hidden from the world."

"It's your world, Chad. Not mine."

He turned and captured both of her arms, forcing her to look at him.

Panic filled her for a moment until she realized his grasp was firm, not bruising.

"It's our world," Chad said. "Our world. I don't want to hear *your world* or *my world*. It's ours."

He looked desperate, and she felt tears sting her eyes. She loved him, and all he'd asked was for her to accompany him to a party. One party. One party for him. "What do they wear?"

Hope filled his eyes, and when he looked down at his hands, he released her arms. "I'm sorry. I hope I didn't hurt you. I didn't mean—"

She gazed into his concerned eyes. "No, you didn't hurt me. You'd never hurt me."

"I know, but—" He waved his hand as if erasing what he'd begun to say, then turned to watch the girls for a moment before turning back. "The men wear suits, and the women wear party dresses."

"Like the one you bought me in Carmel?"

A teasing smile filled his face. "Just like that one."

"And that's why you wanted me to buy it?"

"I had it in mind. I hoped you'd go with me."

How could she say no? She glided her hand over his, her mind filling with his gentle ways, his loving concern for her and Nate. "I'll go with you, Chad. I'd love to go with you."

His mouth curved into a smile.

"I'm not sure about the love-to-go line, but I don't want to go without you, and I know you'll be the most beautiful woman there."

The most beautiful woman there. No man had ever said that to her. The lovely words touched her heart.

thirteen

Felisa looked in the mirror a final time before heading into the main part of the house. The silky dress shimmered in the early evening sunlight, the ripple of coral hues making her think of a glorious sunset. Chad had wonderful taste. She loved the way it wrapped around her and swirled at her calves. She gazed at the dressy tan sandals and clasped the clutch bag in her hand. She prayed the night would pass without incident. If she ever wanted to have the kind of love she dreamed of with Chad, she needed to get past this step. She needed to be accepted in his world.

The thought seemed so impossible.

Her legs trembled as she moved toward the hallway door. She shifted back and took another look at herself in the mirror. She'd tamed her hair, and tonight it fell in soft waves around her shoulders. Lacking jewelry, she'd worn the same imitation gold hoops and necklace she'd worn before. She hoped no one noticed it was costume jewelry.

She pulled in a breath and headed down the hallway, hearing the twins talk with the babysitter, a teenager who'd proven herself very competent. Felisa trusted her to watch Nate, also. When she stepped into the family room, the twins hurried to meet her, sliding their hands along the silky fabric of her dress.

"You look like a princess," Joy said, her voice expressing awe.

Faith only looked at her, speechless.

She saw the sitter eyeing her with an approving look.

"She looks like a queen."

Felisa twirled in the direction of Chad's voice and smiled while her heart danced in her chest. "Thank you," she said, smiling at the girls first and then Chad.

He had his hand behind his back, and she watched him as he strode toward her. When he reached her side, he revealed the package he'd hidden.

Felisa's pulse skipped when she saw the black velvet jewelry box. She couldn't move but stood in front of him looking at the box, then searching his face.

"Don't you want to open it?" Faith asked.

Chad gave Faith a crooked grin, then gazed at Felisa. "Do, please." He edged it closer to her and waited.

When she raised her hands to grasp the box, they were trembling, and she struggled to calm herself and hide her disquiet. "What is it?"

"Open it," he said.

The dialogue had captured the babysitter's interest, and she rose, too, to gape at the gift.

Felisa lifted the lid on the box and gasped. "They're beautiful. So perfect." She gazed at the necklace made of beads trimmed in gold with matching drop earrings. The colors amazed her—rust, muted reds, soft yellow, dark browns, and mottled earth tones. "What is this?"

"Minerals and quartz. Jasper, chalcedony, serpentine."

"Wow!" the teenager said, moving closer. "That's awesome."

"But it's too—"

"I thought it would look lovely with your dress."

"It does. It's beautiful."

"Put it on," Joy said, tiptoeing to look into the box.

"Let me help." Chad took the box from her and released the necklace.

Felisa lifted her hair, unlatched the gold-toned necklace she'd worn, then felt the cool stones fall against her neckline as Chad's warm fingers latched the clasp. His fingers brushed across her nape; then he captured her shoulder and turned her to face him.

"It's beautiful, Felisa. Look in the mirror." He swung his arm toward the wide mirror in the back foyer.

She moved to the hallway mirror in a decorative frame and gazed at her neck in the glass. The vibrant earth-tone colors glinted against her tanned skin, and the coral in her gown was reflected in the various-shaped stones. She'd never seen anything as unique. "I love it. Thank you."

When she turned toward him, he dangled the matching earrings from his fingers. "I'll let you put these on," he said, striding forward to brush back her hair.

She removed her hoop earrings and felt his touch against her cheek as she attached the jewelry to her pierced earlobes. She turned again to the glass to see the effect. She longed to kiss him for the wonderful gift. Saying thank you didn't seem enough.

"You look lovely," he said, his eyes twinkling.

"Thank you," she said again, dropping her other jewelry into the velvet box and setting it on the lamp table.

He bent to kiss the children. "Ready?" he asked, holding his hand toward her.

She kissed the girls and Nate, then clasped Chad's hand and followed him outside.

A soft evening breeze rustled the smooth fabric against her legs. Her heels tapped along the tiles, and the stones around her neck shifted against her skin like a caress. Chad looked handsome in his dark suit and black tie with a tiny stripe of coral. She suspected he'd selected it to match her dress, and the sweet thought pleased her.

She heard his car keys jingle from his pocket, and his hand touched her arm as he opened the passenger door. She slid inside, making sure the skirt of her dress was safe, and then he closed the door. She breathed in the leathery scent of the sedan, mingled with her subtle perfume.

Chad slipped into the driver's seat and closed the door. He guided the key into the ignition, then turned to her. "You look wonderful, Felisa. If anyone looks at you curiously, remember it's as likely envy as anything. I'm proud to have you as my date tonight."

"I'll try," she said, knowing she'd prayed about it since he'd asked her to go.

He turned the key, and the car hummed.

Evening shadows hung on the mountains, and as they drove, dusk fell over the landscape. Felisa filled her mind with good things—her lovely dress, the perfect jewelry, the man at her side whom she'd begun to love. What would the night hold for her? The Lord had never promised to protect her from all of life's sorrows and hurts. Yet He'd promised to be at her side in times of trouble. That was her prayer.

"Where is the party?" Her voice broke the silence.

"Salinas. The rotunda of the Steinbeck Center. It's named after the writer John Steinbeck, who set many of his books in this area. The center is a great place for special events."

She'd heard of John Steinbeck, but as with most places Chad spoke of, she'd never been to the museum. She didn't bother to mention it. She realized by now Chad knew she had experienced so little in her lifetime.

੨

Chad nosed the car down Main Street in Old Town Salinas and parked in the Steinbeck Center parking area. He climbed out and assisted Felisa from the car with his heart racing. She looked unbelievable; yet tension knotted his shoulders. He knew he'd stepped out of the boundaries of what society expected, but they didn't know the woman as he did. He'd wanted so often to talk with Dallas. They'd always been the best of friends, but he'd been afraid. What if Dallas advised him to forget Felisa? What if. . . ? He shook his head. To-night he would put the problem in the Lord's hands. He tilted his head toward the glittering dark blue sky and sent up a silent prayer. *Lord, I put my trust in You.*

He slipped his arm around Felisa's back and guided her into the rotunda. Music greeted them as they entered, and he looked at the guest list and saw the number of his table. When he spotted it, Chad noticed that Brook and Colleen Garner were seated there, too. He cringed with the memory of their last meeting.

He guided Felisa to her chair and felt all eyes on him. "Hello, everyone. I'd like you to meet Felisa Carrillo."

She gave a silent nod and settled into the chair he held for her. "Felisa, you met Brook at the Barnyard after dinner, but I don't think you met Colleen."

Colleen gave a slight arch to her brow and said hello.

Chad finished the introductions, then pulled out his own chair and sat. The conversation seemed strained, but Chad wondered if it was his own tension and not the others'. He wanted to protect Felisa from rude comments, and he hoped no one made any.

The waiter arrived, and he gave their orders, then leaned back, listening to the conversation and inserting comments of his own; but he kept one hand encircling Felisa's. Once in a while he gave it a squeeze, hoping to assure her.

Chad heard his name and pivoted to see his friend Dallas approaching the table. Chad's pulse skipped. Then his spirit soared when he saw the grin on Dallas's face as he eyed Felisa.

He gave Chad a sly look as they shook hands, then turned to Felisa and extended his arm. "I'm Chad's good friend, Dallas Jones."

"This is Felisa Carrillo," Chad said, sorry he hadn't spoken with Dallas sooner.

"Nice to meet you, Felisa." He gave Chad a wink. "At least I thought we were good friends, but he's been noticeably absent. Where have you been?"

Chad winced at his friend's reminder that he had been preoccupied. "Working too hard, I guess. We need to get together. I'll give you a call. How about lunch?"

"Lunch sounds good. Call me tomorrow." Dallas gave him a knowing look, but beneath it, Chad spotted a smile.

"I will. Scout's honor."

"I hope to see you again, Felisa." He grasped Chad's arm and gave it a friendly shake. "Talk with you soon." He bent closer to Chad's ear. "I can't wait to hear how this happened, Romeo."

The waiter cut in, and Chad could only grin at Dallas before he left. But Chad had a good feeling and realized not everyone would condemn him for falling in love with this wonderful woman.

The waiter placed their sparkling water with a twist of lemon beside their plates and moved on with drinks for the others.

Colleen sipped from her fluted glass, and when she put it down she turned her gaze to Chad and then focused on Felisa. "The dress is a lovely color."

"Thank you," Felisa said, her eyes seeking Chad.

"She looks like one of our gorgeous sunsets," Chad said.

"I'm surprised we've never met before," Colleen continued. "How did you and Chad meet?"

He felt Felisa's fingers twitch, and he sensed her panic.

"She is the girls' nanny," Chad said. "They adore her."

"Nanny?" More than one voice responded.

"Yes." He shifted his gaze to Felisa and gave her a smile, hoping that ended the comments.

"But I thought you had an older woman caring for the girls. She wasn't—"

"Mrs. Drake left my employ a while ago. The girls weren't doing well with her, and I think she was frustrated. Felisa has a way with the twins."

"I bet she has," Brook said. He gave Chad a pleasant nod, but his innuendo couldn't be ignored.

Chad swallowed his irritation, and, not wanting to make an issue out of Brook's insinuation, lifted his glass and took a lengthy drink of water. As he did, the music softened, and a sound came from the microphone. To Chad's relief the talk lulled when the president of the association gave his welcome. When he finished, the conversation began again with no other comments.

Felisa seemed to relax, and Chad heard her talking about the twins to the woman next to her. He pushed aside his worries. Other members of the association stopped by to greet them, and he introduced Felisa to pleasant smiles and a few arched brows; but nothing was said, and he thanked the Lord.

The meal passed without incident, and Chad took a deep breath. Things had gone well so far. He'd noticed two of the women at the table responding to Felisa with smiles, and he hadn't missed a couple of the men admiring her. He gave them credit for excellent taste.

Before dessert, Felisa leaned close to his ear and whispered, "I'd like to use the restroom. Which way is it?"

He pointed the way, then rose to pull out her chair. Her dress glimmered when she walked away, carrying her clutch bag. The necklace and earrings he'd given her set off the deep color of her skin and the hues of her gown. She mesmerized him. He tried to hide his grin when he sat down again.

"She's a beautiful woman," Jim Brody said in his ear. "Is she Mexican?"

He gave the man a direct look. "Yes."

The man squirmed in his chair. "Does that bother you? You have Mexicans working in your fields."

Chad noticed the discomfort of the others at the table. "Felisa doesn't work there."

"I know, but—"

Chad held up his hand and scanned the table. "Let's get this out in the open. Felisa's family is from Guadalajara. I hired her as a housekeeper, and before I knew it the twins had fallen in love with her."

"And what about the twins' father?" Colleen gave him a teasing wink.

"That came later," he said, managing a smile. "Since you're all so curious, let me just give you the facts. When Mrs. Drake left, it made sense to ask Felisa to take over the nanny position."

Jim's wife, Della, leaned forward. "She said she has an infant. A boy."

Chad's chest tightened with the pride of a father. "Yes, Felisa's husband died before he knew about the baby. Life has been difficult for her. She needed work, and it all fit together. He's a beautiful little boy."

"A little muchacho, huh?" Brook said as he rose. He rounded the table and squeezed Chad's arm as he leaned down and whispered, "Any of the features look like yours?"

Chad's hands rolled into fists, but he controlled his frustration. "Not one bit. Sorry to disappoint you, Brook."

The man released Chad's arm and vanished behind him. The others watched him leave with uneasy gazes and then returned their focus on Chad.

"What should we make of this?" Jim asked, flashing two arched brows.

"It looks serious to me," Colleen said, a conspiring look

settling on her face. "I think we're witnessing a little romance."

Chad only grinned and didn't respond. The conversation drifted to other topics, and he was pleased they hadn't asked questions while Felisa was present. His feelings and the situation were out in the open now, and most everyone seemed to understand except Brook. Chad scanned the room, looking for him, but he was nowhere in sight.

He felt edgy, wondering if Felisa had gotten lost. The feeling was foolish, he knew. Women often took a long time freshening up, and he realized Felisa was nervous, as well. He turned and watched the doorway. If she didn't return shortly, he would go looking for her.

᪣

Felisa washed her hands and opened her bag. She located her lipstick and glided it across her mouth, then blotted it on a tissue. She continued to admire the necklace and earrings Chad had given her. She'd never received such a lovely gift. Then, having second thoughts, she recalled the gown she wore and the pants and jacket. Those were gifts, too, despite Chad's insistence they were part of a bonus.

Chad felt sorry for her. She could try to pretend it wasn't so, but she knew better. At times she felt sorry for herself, but when she did she pushed it far back in her mind and covered it with God's blessings. Chad's sympathy didn't undermine his feelings. He cared about her, too. She accepted that from the look in his eyes, his tender caresses, and loving words. She couldn't ask for a better gift.

She dropped the lipstick into her handbag and pulled out her comb, caught a few straggly edges, and pushed them back into place. She replaced the comb, then stood back again. *Thank You, Lord. Thank You for tonight and for the past months. You know I love him, and it's in Your hands.*

The restroom door opened as a woman entered. They smiled

at each other, and Felisa drew up her shoulders and caught the door before it closed. As soon as her foot hit the hallway, she saw Brook standing close to the men's room door. Fear skittered up her back. He appeared to be waiting for someone, and she prayed it wasn't her.

She gave him a faint smile as she tried to pass, but his hand clamped on her arm and pulled her back.

"What do you want?" she asked, feeling her heart pounding in her chest.

"Talk," he said.

"Talk? About what?"

"You. . .and me."

She shook her head. What did he mean? Thoughts swirled through her mind. "I'm not interested in changing jobs, Mr.—" She'd forgotten his last name.

He grinned and pulled her against his chest. "I'm not offering you a job, but maybe you'd like a few more pretty little trinkets like these."

He dragged his finger across her necklace, leaving her flesh prickling with fear.

"What do you say?" he asked.

"Please let me go."

She heard the desperation in her voice, but he only laughed.

"Chad Garrison will toss you to the hounds when he's through with you. Don't you know that?"

She cringed at his insinuation. "Chad is a good Christian man. He's kind. Please don't suggest that—"

"Look here, pretty lady. I can be kind, too."

She jerked away from him, but he lashed out for her again. She dodged his hand and raced down the hallway. She couldn't go back inside. She had to get away.

Felisa turned from the reception area and out the front door. Fear tore through her, and she looked over her shoulder to see if he might be following her. Her heels clattered on the concrete sidewalk, and she headed down Main Street, wondering what she would do now. Chad would be worried, but she couldn't go back.

At the cross street, Felisa paused, gasping for breath. She wanted to go home. She opened her handbag and looked inside. She had a few dollars in her purse. Should she take a taxi or try to call Juanita? She didn't know what to do.

❧

Chad's neck ached from twisting toward the door. "Excuse me," he said. "I think Felisa may have gotten lost." He rose and headed toward the outside lobby.

As he stepped through the door he ran into Brook, his face twisted into a scowl, his skin flushed. Brook appeared upset, and his earlier comments about Felisa struck Chad's mind while a warning light triggered in his head.

"Where's Felisa?"

Brook shrugged and tried to pass him.

"Where's Felisa? What have you done?"

"Nothing, man. What's up with you?"

"You said something to her." He imagined the confrontation. "What did you say to her?"

"Neither of you can take a joke."

Chad grasped Brook's arm. "Where is she? What did you do?"

"It was a joke. I offered her a job at my house."

Chad pushed Brook against the wall. "It's time you learned how to treat people with respect, Brook. Would you like someone to make snide comments to your wife? I know Felisa is Hispanic. No one knows that better than I, and you know why? Because she's afraid of people's prejudice. I'm tired of it. Everyone deserves respect. Even you, though it's hard to give it to you when you disrespect others. Felisa's a beautiful woman, inside and out. I've never come on to her. Not even kissed her, though I'm dying to."

Brook drew back, his face filled with disbelief. "Are you serious? You haven't kissed her?"

"That's right."

"Why not?"

Chad's stomach churned. "You disgust me. Because I respect her." He looked at him nose to nose. "Where did she go?"

"I don't know. She left."

"Left?"

"Outside. She ran outside."

Chad's hand dropped from Brook's arm, and he spun around, then raced out the door. What did she plan to do? Where would she go? He halted the questions. She wanted to get away. He hurried to the car, then faltered, his chest aching. She wasn't there. He'd wasted time. He raced back to Main Street and down the sidewalk. "Felisa!" His voice tore through the darkness. He squinted into the dimly lit night. "Felisa!"

Beneath a streetlamp, he saw a flicker of color. His heart hammered as he darted toward it. "Felisa!"

The color stopped and turned toward him. He opened his arms, and Felisa rushed into them.

"It's okay," he said, pressing her head against his shoulder. "You're okay now. I'm so sorry. I'm so sorry."

Her sobs were muffled against his suit jacket. He had never seen her cry this hard before and didn't try to stop her. "I love you, Felisa." The words rolled from his lips like sweet music. Tonight he wanted the whole world to know.

She raised her head, the sound of her sobs diminishing. "I love you, too," she said. "I don't care what people think. I love you."

He drew her into his arms and kissed the salty tears from her cheeks. Her eyes glinted in the light of the streetlamp, and he knew she was speaking with her heart. Later he would tell her that most everyone had teased him about his feelings for her. Eventually everyone would love her just as he did.

Chad captured her lovely face in his hands. He kissed her forehead and the tip of her nose, and when she tilted her mouth upward, he took it as acceptance. He lowered his mouth to hers, tasting of tears, sweet lipstick, and love. *Thank You, Lord. Thank You for this amazing woman.*

fourteen

Ten Months Later

Felisa stood with her arms wrapped around her sister. "Estella, I can't believe it's happening," she said in Spanish.

"I am so happy for you." Her sister gave her a big hug and backed away, tears brimming her eyes. "I don't want to wrinkle your dress."

Felisa shook her head. "The dress isn't as important as you are. I'm so happy you could come here to be my matron of honor."

"I could never have come if Chad hadn't bought my ticket. I'm grateful to him. He's a good man, Felisa. I'm so happy for you."

"Thank you, dearest sister." She brushed tears from her eyes. "I wish Mamá and Papá could be here."

"They would never come so far, but they send their love."

Felisa drew in a lengthy breath. "Will you help me with the mantilla?" She lifted the lacy Spanish veil and handed it to her sister.

Estella fixed it to her hair with combs and arranged it around her shoulders. "You look so beautiful, Felisa."

"Today I feel beautiful." She touched the lovely lace mantilla her mother had sent and lifted her bouquet attached to a delicate fan. She couldn't thank Chad enough for encouraging her to add her Mexican traditions to the wedding. "Is it time?"

"Let me check," Estella said, heading for the door. "You can't see the groom until you come down the aisle." She opened the door a narrow width and slipped out.

Felisa leaned against the wall, reliving the past ten months since Chad had said the most beautiful words in the world—"I love you"—and she'd said them back. She'd opened her heart and let the truth find freedom.

When she'd told Chad the whole story of Brook's sexual harassment, Chad had been furious, but they'd prayed before he confronted Brook about his horrible behavior. When it was over, she and Chad had agreed to put it behind them and pray for Brook instead.

Felisa was so grateful to Juanita, who'd become a good friend, almost like another mother. Today she would sit near the front of the church with Nate, her sweet son who'd grown into such an amazing, smart one-year-old. Once in a while Nate chattered a sound she liked to think was *mama*, but he'd begun to say *dada*, mimicking the girls calling Chad daddy. Not one ounce of envy had entered her thoughts, and she was thrilled for Chad that he'd gained his little son after so much sorrow.

A soft knock sounded on the door, and she clamped her hand over the knob. "Who is it?"

"It's me," her sister said.

"Come in." She scooted out of the way of the door, and Estella ducked inside. "It's time. The girls are so excited. They want to come in and kiss you."

"Let them in," she said, overjoyed at the thought that she would be their mother after today.

Estella opened the door a few inches, and the girls hurried inside, giggling, their pink lace dresses billowing around their knees.

"You both look so pretty," Felisa said, bending down to give them each a hug and a kiss.

"Can we call you Mommy now?" Joy asked.

"I would love that," she said, giving the child's hand a squeeze.

"We love you, Mommy," Faith said.

"I love both of you with all my heart." She forced back the tears. "Now we'd better get out there so I can be your official mommy."

They giggled and hurried out the door with Estella behind them. As Felisa stepped into the hallway and closed the door, her chest filled with joy when she heard the mariachis begin. The wonderful sound of the trumpet, drums, and guitar made her feel at home. The men stood in front at the side, their blue shirts and colorful vests contrasting with the cascades of white roses. She looked ahead of her at the carpet strewn with rose petals, and as she gazed down the aisle she saw Chad and his best man, Dallas Jones, enter from the side.

She watched her sister, then the girls, move down the aisle sprinkling petals, and as the music swelled she took her first step, her eyes only on Chad, whose face glowed with more love than she had ever known.

❧

Chad focused on the aisle, grinning at his beautiful daughters so excited to have a new mother, and then at Juanita holding Nate, who wriggled in her arms to get down. Hearing the boy say *Dada* had captured his heart a hundredfold. Though he wasn't the child's biological father, he would be his father in every other way.

His gaze shifted back to the aisle, and when Felisa stepped onto the carpet of flower petals, his heart swelled until he thought it would burst. The mariachi music filled the room and seemed so right. He'd been grateful to learn the other Mexican wedding traditions so he could please Felisa and let the world know he loved this woman no matter where she was born. God had orchestrated their meeting. He'd sensed it the day he met her.

Felisa seemed to float down the aisle in her cream colored dress with only a single ruffle at the bottom. Her mantilla was held in place by an ornate comb, and she carried a fan adorned with white roses. She'd become his flower, a woman who'd also encouraged him to bloom into the man he was supposed to be.

She reached him, and he took her hands in his for the prayer. Then the pastor brought out thirteen gold coins and spoke. "These coins represent the twelve apostles and Christ. They symbolize Chad's unquestioning trust and confidence in Felisa. When Chad places the coins in Felisa's hands, it is a pledge that all of his goods are placed in her care and safekeeping. Felisa, when you accept these coins, it means you take them with trust and confidence. You accept them unconditionally with total devotion and discretion."

The pastor handed Chad the coins in his cupped hand, and he spilled them into Felisa's. He handed Chad a wooden box, and Felisa put the coins into it and passed it to her sister.

The pastor began, "Chad, do you promise to. . ."

The wonderful words of the marriage ceremony filled Chad's mind and heart as he and Felisa each said, "I do." After the vows, Dallas and Estella bound them together with a cord entwined with orange blossoms.

"This floral lasso is a symbol of fertility and happiness. This loop symbolizes the love that binds you together as you share equally in the responsibility of marriage for the rest of your lives. You are bound together with the Lord as we read in Ecclesiastes 4:12. 'A cord of three strands is not quickly broken.'"

Felisa leaned close to Chad's ear. "God has given us His unfailing love, and forever we will put our trust in Him."

"Forever," he promised her.

Estella and Dallas removed the floral lasso, and the pastor's serious face broke into a smile. "You will now kiss your bride."

Chad gazed at Felisa with misted eyes, his heart singing praise to God. He drew her into his arms, his lips against hers, warm and gentle as a summer breeze. "I love you," he whispered.

"Te amo," she answered.

Her eyes glistened with tears as she stooped to take the twins into her embrace. Chad hurried forward for Nate, the son he'd always wanted and the little boy he loved as his own. When he returned to them with Nate in his arms, he felt total completeness. "My family," he whispered, his eyes blurred with his love. "Thank You, Lord."

A Letter To Our Readers

Dear Reader:

In order that we might better contribute to your reading enjoyment, we would appreciate your taking a few minutes to respond to the following questions. We welcome your comments and read each form and letter we receive. When completed, please return to the following:

Fiction Editor
Heartsong Presents
PO Box 719
Uhrichsville, Ohio 44683

1. Did you enjoy reading *And Baby Makes Five* by Gail Gaymer Martin?
   ❑ Very much! I would like to see more books by this author!
   ❑ Moderately. I would have enjoyed it more if

   _____

   _____

   _____

2. Are you a member of **Heartsong Presents**? ❑ Yes ❑ No
   If no, where did you purchase this book? _____

   _____

3. How would you rate, on a scale from 1 (poor) to 5 (superior), the cover design? _____

4. On a scale from 1 (poor) to 10 (superior), please rate the following elements.

   ____ Heroine   ____ Plot
   ____ Hero   ____ Inspirational theme
   ____ Setting   ____ Secondary characters

5. These characters were special because? _____

_____

_____

6. How has this book inspired your life? _____

_____

_____

7. What settings would you like to see covered in future
   Heartsong Presents books? _____

_____

_____

8. What are some inspirational themes you would like to see
   treated in future books? _____

_____

_____

9. Would you be interested in reading other **Heartsong
   Presents** titles? ❑ Yes ❑ No

10. Please check your age range:
     ❑ Under 18   ❑ 18-24
     ❑ 25-34   ❑ 35-45
     ❑ 46-55   ❑ Over 55

Name _____

Occupation _____

Address _____

City, State, Zip _____

KANSAS WEDDINGS

3 stories in 1

There Kansas women have difficult decisions to make and burdens to bear. Will these women find love despite their handships?

Contemporary, paperback, 352 pages, 5³/₁₆" x 8"

Please send me ____ copies of *Kansas Weddings*. I am enclosing $6.97 for each.
(Please add $3.00 to cover postage and handling per order. OH add 7% tax.
If outside the U.S. please call 740-922-7280 for shipping charges.)

Name_____

Address _____

City, State, Zip _____

To place a credit card order, call 1-740-922-7280.
Send to: Heartsong Presents Readers' Service, PO Box 721, Uhrichsville, OH 44683

Hearts♥ng

Any 12 Heartsong Presents titles for only $27.00*

CONTEMPORARY ROMANCE IS CHEAPER BY THE DOZEN!

Buy any assortment of twelve *Heartsong Presents* titles and save 25% off the already discounted price of $2.97 each!

*plus $3.00 shipping and handling per order and sales tax where applicable.
If outside the U.S. please call 740-922-7280 for shipping charges.

HEARTSONG PRESENTS TITLES AVAILABLE NOW:

(If ordering from this page, please remember to include it with the order form.)